ANDRE GONZALEZ

Followed Away

For Arielle, Felix, and Selena

"It's so much darker when a light goes out than it would have been if it had never shone."

— John Steinbeck

Contents

Free Download - A Poisoned Mind

Read a spinoff story about the Exalls for free by CLICKING HERE. Check out A Poisoned Mind today!

A POISONED
MIND
ANDRE GONZALEZ

1

Chapter 1

The nightmares didn't stop for two weeks. They were nothing but jumbled images of life before Plan D had been so seamlessly executed. Images of his friends, his mom and dad, his grandmother, Colonel Griffins. And of course, his best friend, Brian, infected with gray skin and the evil ways of the Exalls. Ever since the bloody scene in the middle of the D.C. freeway, Kyle Wells could simply close his eyes and replay the horrific events, watching his own bullet tear through his friend. Then a few minutes later, watching another bullet catch Colonel Griffins in the throat and dropping him like a sack of potatoes.

That was all fine and well, something Kyle could manage until he'd meet with a psychiatrist—if any were still alive. But the nightmares flashed through his mind like a demented highlight reel of doom. There was still zero communication possible to the outside world, and they still hadn't cleared their path out of the underground offices that had been home for the last two weeks.

The Crew knew what to expect when they returned to the world above: a demolished country, all signs of life wiped away.

Kyle, by far the most junior of the surviving members, had the most questions about Plan D and why it had to be carried out.

It was strictly a decision by the president. The Exalls had reached a population count that severely threatened the livelihood of all Americans. Ever since the Crew had come into existence in the 1960s, they determined it would be better—and safer—for the entire country's population to be wiped off the map should they reach this point. Letting the Exalls run rampant would spread death and doom faster than a plague. It would cause every citizen to hide in fear and watch from their windows as the alien species slowly took their society over.

The Exalls had no mercy, no interest in holding humans captive. They would murder any human in sight, a means to satisfy their starvation for ruling the entire planet. Either way, the population of the United States would be killed, but they considered it better to do on the government's terms, where a follow-up plan was in place to repopulate after eliminating the threat of the Exalls. They also knew the Exalls' interest in Earth was mainly because of the established infrastructure. With a major country completely wiped out, this would leave them no choice but to give up their hopes of inhabiting the planet.

"What's going on in the rest of the world?" Kyle had asked after two days of settling into the new norm of digging through the parking garage with the morning crew, and strategizing in the afternoons for that special moment when they returned to the outside world.

"We don't know for sure, since we can't communicate with anyone," Major Ortiz said. He was the most senior of the remaining twelve Crew members, an athletic Hispanic man in his early fifties. His experience made him the unofficial leader of their squad, and no one had any arguments against it. He was well-respected, even considered a potential replacement for Colonel Griffins. "We have highly classified information that is supposed to be released to our allies in case of Plan D. Assuming it all went according to plan, other countries may have had to follow suit. It all depends on what sort of Exall activity they've seen."

"So the entire world could be completely decimated?" Kyle asked.

Ortiz nodded slowly as he sat down behind a table and opened a can of peas. "Possible. Not likely, but I can't tell you for sure, kid."

They had many conversations like this over the course of two weeks. They discussed everything from plans of finding the president, studying their food supply, and what they needed to do once back in the world.

Their initial task included a sweep of the D.C. area. They did not expect the metro areas to have any survivors, but the rural might—and likely would. It was impossible to bomb every single farm across the country, especially in the Midwest plains where some weren't within five hundred miles of a major city. They expected little along the East coast, and hoped to encounter survivors as they made their way west.

Kyle had pleaded with Major Ortiz that they needed to stop in Larkwood, Colorado—that *he* needed to drop by his father's home and check on something. Sandra the Exall could help them. At the very least, Kyle knew there were answers buried in the file cabinets within the secret laboratory. He planned to keep his secret close to his chest, and would have to decide the right time to tell Major Ortiz.

"We've got one more hour," Ortiz told their squad. Of the twelve remaining, they had split into three squads of four, each rotating shifts of eight hours digging, eight hours of sleep, and eight hours of free time—which consisted more of planning to keep their minds occupied. They had discovered after a couple of days that free time really meant worry time, each soldier pondering over if their own families and friends had survived the attacks. For Kyle, only his father would have had the knowledge to recognize what was happening. For some of the more senior Crew members, though, they had a few more relatives with knowledge of the secret. But that guaranteed nothing. Travis could have been at the grocery store for all Kyle knew, leaving him no chance of making it back to safety. They didn't exactly announce that bombs were being dropped, seeing as they meant the plan to leave as few survivors as possible.

"One hour until paradise," Camille Monroe said. She served the Crew as a captain, and had worked in the technology department before all the electricity had gone out. She had been the first to inform the survivors that the backup generator was only meant to power their underground offices for one month. Camille had griped every day before their digging shift would begin, something they each looked forward to as she always went on a similar rant. "How would you like to survive the end of the world? As a bonus prize for your survival, how would you like to dig your way out to make sure you actually live? Makes perfect sense, dear government. How did you come up with such a brilliant idea out of your endless wisdom?"

Camille had grown extra bitter and sardonic since the bombs had dropped. Realizing her role as one of the few surviving women set aside by the Crew, she had her fertility tested every month to ensure she could help with the last phase of Plan D: repopulating the country. She had brought it up on day one, a feminist explosion about the importance of women in the military. It hadn't been discussed since, but they all knew it picked at her mind with each passing day.

"You finish our route yet, Franzen?" Ortiz asked, crumbling up a napkin and throwing it at Bernard Franzen, a lieutenant who had been leaning back in a recliner with his hat lowered over his eyes.

Bernard caught the napkin in his lap and tossed it aside, grinning as he sat up and lifted his hat. "Can't a man take a nap without being harassed any more? Our route is done, Major."

The three squads would each cover certain routes once they broke out, sweeping the country from coast to coast in search of any survivors—whether human or Exall. According to the initial numbers generated by Plan D projections, approximately 30,000 American residents were expected to survive the attacks. The first phase of recovery, which would easily span the course of three months, was to drive around the country in search of these survivors and gather all of their demographic information. While the plans for beginning the repopulation of the country—and potentially the world—were at least a year out, they needed to know what resources they had available.

Bernard was 32 years old and only had his sights set on killing Exalls. He had risen through the ranks as one of the best soldiers they'd ever seen. During the battle on the freeway, he had run toward the incoming Exalls and showered bullets upon the aliens like Tony Montana. They shot back at him, but his body armor deflected everything, leaving him unscathed when so many never made it home that night. Being trapped underground had driven him stir-crazy, and he'd randomly lash out at the most minor of inconveniences. On day five, when he found the peanut butter container empty, he ripped out the drawer of silverware in their kitchen and chucked it across the room, muttering every known curse word in the English language.

"We have the easiest route," Bernard said. "A straight shot down I-70 takes us all the way to central Utah. Twenty-five hours to that point, assuming the roads are clear the whole way."

"We're taking I-70?!" Kyle jumped out his seat, his heartbeat suddenly spiking. "We're going to Denver?"

"That we are," Bernard replied with another grin.

"Relax, Wells," Ortiz said. "Just because we're going that direction doesn't mean we'll be able to stop. We're at the mercy of what we find on the way. We could always have to detour and end up nowhere near Denver—I don't want you to get your hopes up."

"Major, please, we *have* to stop. I promise it's for a good reason." Kyle pleaded like a teenager begging to go out with his friends on a school night.

Ortiz held up his thick hand. "We'll do our best. I think we each have a stop on the way where we'd like to check on things from our personal life, but we can't promise anything. And you may not like what we find—that's likely, in fact."

Kyle fell silent, sinking back into his chair. Inevitably, he'd have to tell Major Ortiz about the big secret sooner. If he didn't, they just might drive past Denver and never look back. The only thing holding him back was fear they would kill Sandra. But he knew there had to be answers buried in that room. Answers that might help them restore the world.

2

Chapter 2

"I think another day and we'll be out," Major Ortiz grunted, swinging a pickaxe into a boulder of concrete. The Crew's offices were unharmed six levels below, the damage done at ground level, where the remains of the Pentagon had crumbled on top of the parking garage exit.

Yesterday had been a cause for celebration, as the squad led by Ortiz struck the blow that let a lone stream of light seep through the cracks. It was a visual finish line that had yet to appear after two weeks of blindly digging. Camille complained the Crew didn't leave them any heavy machinery to plow their way out, baffled that they actually had to dig by hand. Even though she didn't say it, seeing the daylight provided hope, as her negative comments had reduced to a minimum for the rest of the day.

"Tomorrow *will* be our last day of digging, so help me God," Bernard said, shoveling the debris aside where many mounds had formed from all of their work. "How does that sound, Captain?"

"Sounds marvelous," Camille replied. "Then I'll be off to the first remaining bar I can find and will drink them dry."

"We will definitely celebrate," Ortiz added, his bulging muscles bringing the axe down once more. Kyle had caught himself stopping to watch Major Ortiz on a couple of instances. The man was a machine, a human jackhammer who never seemed to run out of power. He could swing the axe for eight hours straight, only stopping for thirty minutes to eat a quick meal and chug a single bottle of water.

Ortiz and Kyle both worked with the axe, while Bernard and Camille scooped and spread their piles outward. Kyle had to stop at least once an hour to catch his breath and give his arms a momentary rest.

"Have you even had alcohol, Wells?" Bernard asked with a wide grin, earning a chuckle from everyone else.

"I've had some drinks with my parents—wine and beer."

"We have lots to teach you, kid," Bernard said. "First bottle of Scotch is on me."

"Franzen, you shouldn't promote underage drinking," Ortiz said, still hammering away.

Bernard let out an exaggerated laugh. "I didn't realize we still had laws, Major. Until we ever get word from the president, you're the highest-ranking official in the United States. So if you want Wells to have a drink, then he can have a drink."

"The president is still in charge, even if we have no communication with him. Plan D calls for very specific actions from the Oval Office, and that's what we're following."

Bernard shook his head as he kept shoveling.

"Besides," Ortiz continued. "Is drinking all you want to do when we get out? I want to just walk around the park and enjoy nature. Our Outside Room hasn't worked in two weeks."

"Not sure there's much of nature left out there, Major,"

Camille said.

They had spent an entire two days trying to get the outside cameras working. They were teased with what appeared to be an attempted connection, but it never worked. None of them knew what to expect. All the plans suggested that a deserted world awaited once they broke through: demolished buildings and monuments, no trace of human life. But there was still the likelihood of survivors. What were they up to? If any Exalls survived, would they have slipped away into hiding, or roamed the streets raising hell?

"Birds always survive," Ortiz said. "All the way back to the dinosaurs. Even if a walk through the park is actually a walk through smoldering buildings, as long as the birds are singing, I'll be fine."

"Such a romantic," Camille said with a chuckle. "You gonna plant some flowers while you're at it?"

They all shared a laugh and kept working. Their bond had strengthened in the past few days. Ortiz had opened up, peeling the layers off his stern exterior, and promptly causing the rest of the squad to poke fun at each other. Even Kyle, who felt like an outcast for being the youngest, had grown closer with all three of them. They teased him the most, but he understood it all came from a place of respect. Nothing changed the fact he was the grandson of a legend, and had excelled in his own right upon joining the Crew. He was the youngest member ever to have fought in a live battle against Exalls, an experience typically reserved for members in their late thirties.

Major Ortiz had pulled Kyle aside on their second day underground and told him he specifically wanted him on his squad. While he would have been in excellent hands with any of the three squads, Ortiz believed Kyle would benefit the most from being on his team. As the major, Ortiz chose the best squad and most experienced of the remaining survivors. Kyle would only expand his knowledge by rubbing elbows with the best. Ortiz told Kyle he had the making of a future colonel for the Crew, and if he put his mind to it, could do anything within the government and military.

It was rare for someone to leave the Crew for another branch, but when a request was made, their name was always at the top of the list. The Crew was heavily considered the best of the best, thanks to their secretive and stringent recruitment process.

Kyle used to think of the future regularly, but when the bombs dropped, all of his focus shifted to survival. The future no longer provided hope, but a gnawing fear of what the world looked like, what had happened to his family and friends, and what would happen with Sandra once they arrived in Larkwood.

"What is it you want so badly in Denver?" Bernard asked, as if reading his mind. His tone shifted to a much more serious one, another sign Kyle had learned to pick up when his new team meant business. Ortiz had asked this same question in private, but Kyle only gave vague responses.

"I've got something very personal that I need to check on," Kyle said, fighting to make sure his voice wasn't wavering like his arms were. Whenever the mere thought of Sandra popped into his head, his guts swirled. An open discussion about the secret was nearly unbearable.

"Like a person or a possession?"

This question caught Kyle off guard, as he didn't know the best way to answer. Fortunately, their continued digging concealed his hesitation. "A possession. Something my grandma left for me—just want to make sure it's okay, you know?"

"Absolutely I do. I've got something similar, too. My dad was living in St. Louis. I retired him from his job when he was fifty—the beauty of these Crew salaries. Anyway, one of his bucket list items was to build a classic car from scratch. So I gave him funds to start the project, and he never looked back. He built a 1966 Ferrari 330 GT. Spent weeks on the phone calling all over the world to get parts shipped to St. Louis. It took him an entire year, but he did it. The car is stunning: cherry-red paint, black leather interior. He'd take it cruising around town and turned heads. I'd never seen my dad so proud of something he created—he was a carpenter and made lots of things with his hands. It was really his pride and joy, and as a thank you, he wanted to leave it for me when he passed."

"You don't think he survived the bombings?" Kyle asked, everyone now having stopped digging to listen.

"Not likely. I had a small bunker built for him, but he told me he'd never use it. He insisted that he'd rather not live in a world where a government would wipe out its own people. I can only hope he had a last-second change of heart, but I'm not holding my breath. If he is in that bunker, that'll be the true gift. If not, I only hope that car is okay—it's the one thing I can hold on to forever."

The glistening of a tear streamed down Bernard's face as he sniffled and looked down to wipe it away.

Major Ortiz spoke up. "Look, Wells. We all have stories like this. We all have something we need to check on at home. That's why we have the route we do. My promise to each of you is to make every reasonable attempt possible to stop by your homes. You three have it easier though—my home is San Francisco, our final stop. I've got a long way before getting to where I need, but that won't hinder us from making our stops on the way."

They all nodded, remaining silent. Camille's stop was in Dayton, Ohio. She had been a fairly closed book, however, and hadn't spoken openly about what might await at home.

Major Ortiz returned to swinging his pickaxe, prompting everyone else to follow suit and return to work. He didn't need to say it, but they all knew the faster they dug, the sooner they'd be visiting their hometowns.

3

Chapter 3

Robert Chapman sat on his front lawn, a flask of whiskey in one hand, a slow-burning cigarette in the other. After sixty-two years on this planet and a lifetime of pain, he never thought twice about lighting up and having a few puffs. His home lay in ruins behind him, a mere pile of wood that had once housed his life's memories.

The bombing of his city—and the entire country—hadn't traumatized him. He expected it, building a life of preparation for the inevitable execution of Plan D. When his wife passed away ten years earlier after a vicious battle against cancer, all of his family and friends thought he had lost his mind. Some called him a lunatic. Others insisted the tragedy had removed him from reality. His own sister called him a conspiracy theorist, a term meant to insult him, but one he embraced.

They were perhaps right in their accusations, considering Robert had article clippings and internet printouts all over his bedroom that discussed a potential alien species roaming the country. There had been too many cancer deaths in the area with no logical explanation, prompting Robert to fall down a rabbit hole that kept making sense the more he read.

Most, if not all, conspiracy theories derived from people's imaginations, or at least a lack of understanding why certain things happened. They ran even more rampant in the United States where unchecked news outlets and social media made it easier to convince people of your off-the-wall theory. In a country where people believed the 9/11 attacks and the Kennedy assassination were inside jobs, Robert found an audience when he started speaking of an alien species roaming the world, slithering in the background like a snake waiting to pounce on its prey.

He wasn't the first to discuss aliens—he had attracted many followers who visited places like Area 51 and Roswell, New Mexico—but as he looked around at what used to be his neighborhood, he believed he was the last. And that made his theory a true conspiracy.

Even when his inner circle came crashing down around him, Robert stuck to his truth. He wasn't pulling theories out of his ass—he had lived them. The saddest part was knowing that his new friends—his fellow conspiracy theorists—were a bunch of frauds. Had they actually believed the message he was preaching, maybe they would still be alive. Some admitted to having underground bunkers. Most weren't deep enough to survive the bombs, while others hadn't opened theirs in years. He had told anyone who survived the attacks to meet at his property, and it had now been two weeks without seeing a single soul pass by his block.

Robert was alone—had been for years—but never felt *lonely*. It was a fine line, but one he had grown to master in the years following his wife's death. He didn't need companionship. That's what his research was for. Robert could see the differences between himself and other conspiracy theorists he had met. The others lacked any self-awareness, some simply didn't give a shit what others thought. But Robert understood the toll his beliefs took on his family and friends. He didn't fault anyone for cutting him out of their life. What he had learned in the two weeks since the bombs was that his open-mindedness had saved him. His ability to look at things from all perspectives—not just a few, but *all.*

This was something he had instilled in his son during his high school years. "You can learn all the things you want," he had told him one evening as they tossed a baseball back and forth. "But if you can't consider another man's perspective, you're doomed to fail. And not just *his* perspective, but the perspective of that same man's friends and enemies. Only then will you have a complete picture to make a sound judgment."

His son, Gavin, had been struggling with a classmate determined to make his life a living hell. Thanks to Robert's advice, Gavin was able to piece together a much larger puzzle by speaking with friends of the bully, eventually learning that he had been struggling with the death of his little brother over summer break. Gavin found common ground with the death of his own mother, and the two became best friends.

It was at this moment when Robert realized his son would be just fine in this world. He had always shared the findings of his research on the alien species, but never forced his son into believing it. He'd eventually come around on his own, assuming he maintained his open mind.

It wasn't until Gavin moved to Denver for college when he started connecting dots on his own. There had long been a conspiracy theory surrounding Denver International Airport—dozens, in fact—that suggested the airport was built above an underground lair where world leaders could meet in the event of an apocalypse. Gavin had taken a part-time job at the airport, well before learning about the theories, but eventually arrived to some conclusions of his own.

He'd keep updating his father with new findings over six months on the job, until they abruptly fired him for entering a restricted area. They asked for no explanation and demanded he leave the airport immediately, not even allowing him to gather his belongings. As far as job performance, Gavin had a clean record, so the firing led him to suspect that he had gotten a bit too close to one of the secrets.

Robert played through these events in his mind, wondering what the airport looked like today. If the theory was correct, did they even bother bombing it? Did the rest of the world even know about the Exalls or Plan D? Throughout his research, he never found evidence that suggested they did. If this was all a big American secret, then what was the rest of the world doing these past two weeks? Surely someone—Canada, most likely—would have at least sent someone to come take a look.

Robert believed it impossible that other countries didn't have their own version of an alien hunting department. Hell, there was evidence of the Exalls roaming the land in other countries, but the reports he had read showed only U.S. Crew members had been involved with locating—and executing, in some instances.

He was perhaps the most knowledgeable person outside of D.C. regarding the Exalls, likely the only person who even knew about them and understood why the entire country had been demolished within the matter of an hour. But none of that mattered if he was the only person still alive. Sure, his son likely survived in Denver, but how the hell was he supposed to get there? He had driven fifty miles in every direction in search of survivors, and while he didn't encounter any major obstacles on the road, it was irresponsible to assume the entire thousand-mile stretch to Denver would be just as clear.

He had seen some of the craters in the ground around Dayton. Where a grocery store once stood was nothing but a ten-foot deep hole, not so much as a single banana having survived what was surely a direct strike. A thick, brown haze had clung to every air particle in town for the first week, many structures still smoldering as others finished their eventual collapse. Breathing outside of the bunker proved difficult during that time, leaving Robert trapped underground for most of the week.

Once the haze cleared and the sun shone brightly again, Robert started his evening ritual of sitting on his front lawn, smoking and drinking without a care in the world. He stocked his food and water in the bunker, enough to last him six months. His only worry was running out of booze and tobacco, but he couldn't justify sacrificing precious storage space for items that didn't keep him alive. Although, he liked to argue, the alcohol kept him sane. None of the liquor stores or tobacco shops in Dayton had survived the attacks, so a venture down to neighboring Kettering would be due soon, and hopefully at least one store survived where he could rummage for alcohol.

For now, he watched as the sun started its descent behind the horizon, wondering how many survivors were out there. How many Exalls. He had guns and ammunition ready to fight whatever might come his way, but he prayed it wouldn't come to that. Hopefully, these attacks achieved their purpose in destroying the entirety of the Exalls. But if he had survived, who was to say that even a single Exall didn't?

"I know you're out there," he said to the sunset, taking another drag from the cigarette. He exhaled and flicked the butt away, gazing, knowing he'd have to muster up the energy at some point to make the trek to Denver and find his son. Robert closed his eyes and said a quick prayer for Gavin.

4

Chapter 4

It ended up taking four more days, but the entire group of surviving Crew soldiers gathered around as the squad led by Major Ortiz did the honor of breaking down the final debris that trapped them inside.

"Ladies and gentlemen, the world as we know it no longer exists on the other side of this rock," Major Ortiz reminded them.

Light poured through the gaps and holes, now big enough for a small child to crawl through. The anticipation grew palpable as Ortiz picked up his ax and returned to the debris, pausing a moment to stare it down. They all watched in silence as he swung three times, the third being the final blow that caused the uppermost chunk to roll down the hill of fallen debris like a small boulder. He hopped aside to let it pass as everyone cheered, high-fiving and hugging each other.

"Good shit, Major!" one soldier yelled, grins wide on all of their faces.

Once the celebration died down, their attention returned to Major Ortiz, tossing aside the pickaxe like a cocky baseball player after a home run. He crossed his arms and faced his team, a rare grin plastered across his face. "I know this is exciting, and none of us thought this moment would ever come. But remember, this is all part of a grand plan. We were *supposed* to be trapped, and now we move to the next phase. I know you've all been preparing: we have our routes set, our meals packed and planned, and most importantly, our weapons ready.

"I've said it before, and I'll say it again. We must remain diligent once we step outside. None of our technology works—it's safe to assume the power grid has been disrupted across the country. If there are surviving Exalls, which I expect there will be a few, we'll be fighting them blind. Under no circumstances should you grow complacent. Consider the Exalls a threat at all times of day, no matter where you are. Even after you sweep a town, don't assume it's safe and let your guard down. We are *months*, if not years, away from being able to sit back and relax. Treat every day and each new town as a potential threat, especially in rural areas, since they hit those the least. Any questions?"

"When are we leaving?" a soldier asked.

"Whenever you and your squad are ready. My team and I are leaving first thing in the morning. That reminds me, it's best to not travel at night since we don't have our tracking devices. It's much easier for those gray bastards to sneak up on us at night. Be sure to find shelter, or at least a good stopping point before nightfall. Now, who's ready to head outside and look around?"

The dozen of them roared, promptly stepping forward, eager to see the light of day for the first time in weeks. The group naturally split into their squads, gathering and chatting with each other at the base of the rubble. It was a short climb, no more than a foot in elevation, but everyone followed behind Major Ortiz as he led the way.

The Crew's offices were six levels below ground, but the debris had collapsed on the ground-level entrance. They had all ridden in Humvees up to the ground level, going through the spiral road that connected all levels of the underground parking garage. They needed more digging to fit the vehicles through, but for now the hole fit at least three people at once.

They filed through, climbing up the hill and stepping foot outside, the sun blaring above, causing many of them to shield their eyes as they adjusted.

Complete silence swallowed the entire world around them. They were only a couple hundred yards away from the Richmond Highway, but not a single car motored by. Fencing and tall shrubbery normally concealed the Pentagon from the rest of the area, but that had all been demolished, leaving an unobstructed view and path across the highway where the Potomac River flowed, abandoned from the usual crowds of tourists that cruised or fished. Planes taking off and landing had been constant at the nearby Reagan National Airport, but the airport itself was gone, and not a plane was in sight.

While Major Ortiz expected the world to look nothing like what he had known his entire life, the flatness of everything caught him off guard the most. He pulled out a pair of binoculars and scanned the area. The Pentagon had been its own little world, despite being in the middle of a bustling area. But now, he could see at least ten miles in any direction. Gone were the rows of white marble gravestones at the neighboring Arlington National Cemetery, the Washington Monument, Lincoln Memorial, and U.S. Capitol. The area of the White House at least had rubble where the iconic house once stood, a tattered American flag standing crookedly out of the debris.

Ortiz lowered the binoculars as his throat tensed shut, unable to even swallow the spit pooling in his mouth. The rest of the group stood in silence, gradually spinning around to absorb the reality of the new, wide-open world. Looking back at where they had dug out from, what was once the Pentagon was a mere mound of gray debris.

"It's *too* quiet," Bernard said, voice wavering.

His comment prompted them to all look up to the sky, clear except for a couple of clouds looming in the east. No planes, no birds, just silence.

"Keep in mind, all major cities were to be reduced to ashes," Ortiz said. "There is surely wildlife roaming the plains in the country, but expect nothing else to have survived here in D.C."

He spun around to find two soldiers—a husband and wife duo by the names of Louise and John Akins—crying, embracing each other. They had lived through a stillbirth last year for what would have been their first child. Ever since, there seemed to have been constant trauma both in their lives and the world. They sobbed, prompting their two squadmates to glide over and embrace them in a team hug.

There was no denying the intensity of the situation. And even though the air was crystal clear—now that the smoke had settled—it still felt difficult to breathe, a macabre destiny pressing against each of their lungs.

"This is . . . chilling," Camille said, holding out her arms to show them covered in gooseflesh on what was at least an eighty-degree day. "How were we even capable of doing this?"

"Number one military in the world," Ortiz said. "Biggest defense budget. This is what all that buys you."

Everyone had gradually formed small huddles with their

squads, perhaps a subconscious form of comfort after having spent the last two weeks with their particular group almost exclusively.

"How exactly are we supposed to rebuild all of this?" Bernard asked, his voice still unsteady. "There's no way we have the resources to pull this off."

"We do," Ortiz said, gazing around through his binoculars. "All the resources remain. We're still ahead of the times when humans had to create everything from scratch. We have water lines, sewage, electric lines. It's all still here—we just have to repair it. That's why we have to sweep the country and find everyone we can. The twelve of us have no chance of doing it on our own."

"What about the president's team?" Bernard asked. "How are we supposed to get ahold of them? I'd imagine he had a sizable group surrounding him."

"I honestly have no idea. Supposedly there are bunkers all around the country meant to house the president. Colonel Griffins might have known, but he never mentioned anything."

"POTUS will be just fine," Camille cut in. "We have our job to do, just like they have theirs. I'm sure at some point we'll cross paths, but for now we need to focus on our mission."

Bernard shifted his stance, turning away from Camille. Whenever she got into a productive mood, she never hesitated to roll over anyone standing in her way. They were all still trying to grasp the reality of this unknown world, but she was ready to get right to business.

"I know we have lots to speculate about," Ortiz said. "But we have a plan to follow, and we *must* follow it to the finest detail. Anything else outside of that scope is irrelevant."

"Like stopping in each of our towns to check on things?"

Camille asked, her tone daring Ortiz to open this debate with her. "Was that written in the plans for when they bombed the entire country? Make sure each survivor gets to go home to collect their sentimental belongings?"

Ortiz scratched his head out of frustration. "No, *Captain*, it was not in the plans. I also have the authority to adjust plans as necessary. The whole point of stopping by our homes is to check for survivors. We all have family members with knowledge of The Crew, and therefore, may have taken cover in underground bunkers. I have authorized everyone to stop by their homes for this very reason. It's our most likely chance of finding survivors—which *is* our primary focus for the next six months. Are we clear?"

Even though he was a major, and currently the highest-ranking official in the government—until the president made his presence known—Ortiz rarely shouted or took a tone with his team. But he certainly didn't lack the ability to exhibit his authority when needed. His tone toward Camille was both powerful and dismissive, and she snickered as she turned away from him, mumbling that she was indeed clear on his instruction.

Ortiz returned his attention to the group at large, booming his voice as they had all broken into their own conversations. "I think that settles it for now. Let's head back inside and prepare for our departures. Tomorrow is the start of forever in this new world. I suggest we all get a good night's rest, because we don't know how common of an event that will be once we start our trips across the country. If anyone has any pressing matters to discuss with me, please do so before lights out at 9 P.M. Otherwise, I'll see you all in the morning before we head our separate ways."

5

Chapter 5

At 8 A.M. they drove out of the garage and circled the entire Pentagon property. They didn't expect any survivors, considering everyone was already dead before the bombs dropped. They were officially starting their mission of driving through every city they passed, sweeping the rubble for any scarce signs of life.

Major Ortiz wanted to check two areas in D.C. before heading west, so they first stopped at the location of the White House, arriving to an eerie scene of not only the house demolished, but all the perimeter fencing and lawns as well. A lone security booth remained, half collapsed and leaning along the pathway that led to the south entrance. The armed gate was nowhere in sight, so they drove right up to the edge of the debris.

It had only been weeks since Kyle and his father sat in the Oval Office and signed the contract to join the Crew. Now he craned his neck for a view of the crumbled building.

"All that history just flushed down the toilet," Bernard said. "Like it never happened."

"If the president authorized the bombings, why would they

bomb the White House?" Kyle asked.

"The purpose was to remove any major landmarks that might attract a gathering," Major Ortiz said. "Keep in mind there are survivors. In time, they would naturally flock to big public areas just to see if they can find others. This way there is nowhere for people to flock—that's our job to round them up and let them know the next phases of this plan."

Camille stared out the window and remained silent. She hadn't spoken a word since they left, her leg bouncing during the entire drive. She seemed like she might jump out of the Humvee at any moment and make a run for whatever was occupying her mind.

Ortiz pulled out a paper that showed a blueprint of the White House. "According to this, the president's bunker should be just thirty feet from us." He looked up to the rubble, seeing nothing but mounds of burnt wood and shattered glass. The U.S. flag flapped in the distance, about another two hundred feet deeper into the mess.

"Doesn't look like they've made their way out yet," Bernard said.

"I don't believe they're supposed to have," Ortiz replied. "The president will probably remain underground for at least two months. The plan is to allow us time to sweep the country once. By then we should be on the West Coast to start our routes back this way."

"But if there's no communication, then what's the point?" Kyle asked. "Whether or not everything is clear, we have no way of relaying that information."

Ortiz tossed up his hands and shrugged. "I don't make the rules, I only follow them."

"Where else are we going?" Bernard asked, his tone dismissing the White House as a lost cause. Clearly no one was rising from these ashes.

"Andrews," Ortiz said. "We should check if there are any jets that survived—they could help us speed up our current mission."

He was referring to Andrews Air Force Base, a thirty-minute drive southeast from the White House. It was home to Air Force One and other high-profile jetliners. They assumed the bombings would have originated from this location, so Ortiz wanted to look and see if they had bombed themselves, or at least find a functioning jet to use for travel. Whoever had dropped the bombs across the country had to land somewhere afterward, and he prayed it was at Andrews.

"That's actually not a bad idea," Camille spoke up for the first time, remaining monotone. "They'll need something nearby to fly the president to wherever he's going once he's out of the bunker. Are you suggesting we steal a jet from the base?"

"It's not stealing if we're on the same team."

"We're *not* on the same team, Major. The Air Force likely took their orders without questioning anything. If they still have their jets, they'll be there guarding them. And you really think they're going to let a group of self-proclaimed alien hunters take one for a spin? They'll shoot us."

"You're thinking too much into this. We all have government-issued ID's. We can speak to them about what exactly happened. It won't take much for us to prove ourselves."

"Major, no one else knows about us. Clueless. Not even the Space Force is familiar with what we do—we're completely under the radar as far as the other branches of military are concerned. They have no reason to believe a word you say."

"We're all alive, all wear the same uniforms. We have information, and now that the secret is out, we can talk about everything, including our office below the Pentagon. And who knows, they might actually have a direct line of communication to the president, who can certainly vouch for us."

Camille bit her bottom lip, clearly holding back her thoughts.

"We're just checking," Bernard said. "There's probably nothing there. I doubt they would bomb the White House and *not* Andrews. They gotta have a new, remote location where all of those jets landed afterward."

They had passed Capitol Hill, rolling down Pennsylvania Avenue to find everything flattened. Familiar restaurants, mom-and-pop shops, and even the nearby Nationals Park were all gone. Major Ortiz had to weave through tipped over vehicles and mounds of rubble, zipping through the silent capital city like a labyrinth. Despite what seemed like constant obstacles, nothing ever blocked the entire road.

It also helped that the Humvee could drive over telephone poles and smashed cars.

"This is so fucked up," Kyle said. "We're just driving over these dead bodies. These innocent people who were just minding their business and never saw it coming. Do any of you feel guilty for surviving this?"

They rode for a few seconds in silence until Bernard spoke up. "Look, Wells, I know this is the most extreme situation that has ever happened to you. It is for all of us. You've got to understand the line between empathy and guilt. *You* didn't bomb these innocent people. *You* didn't authorize it. Hell, you didn't even know it was happening until it did. None of us did.

"There's no reason to feel guilty. These people were eventually going to be killed and transformed into weapons against us. Our country was going to be burned to the ground one way or another. We just did it ourselves with a specific plan in place. So yes, feel empathy toward these lost lives, but not guilt. Honor them by helping rebuild our land, Exall free. No more threats, no more senseless attacks. When they crashed into your middle school, that was only the beginning. We saw how reckless they were being these last few months, and that was with small numbers. It reached the point where we couldn't stop it without bombing the shit out of all of them."

Kyle stared out the window as they continued through chaos. "How do we know it worked? What if some Exalls survived and they've been infecting the other survivors we're supposed to be on the lookout for? There could already be thousands of them waiting for us in one of these cities—we'd have no chance."

Kyle's words prompted more silence, having struck a nerve, as they all sulked in their thoughts. He had these concerns for the past few days. He had witnessed firsthand, on multiple occasions, how ruthless the Exalls were. The thought of even a couple of them running rampant across the country sent chills up his back. They had turned his best friend into his biggest enemy, forcing Brian to lunge at Kyle with murder in his non-beating, undead heart.

Major Ortiz cleared his throat. "There will definitely be some who survived. That's not the problem. First off, we don't know if they will still try to infect other humans. The goal was to send them into hiding, and force them off the planet. It's very possible any surviving Exalls have already left during these last two weeks. They wanted Earth for its infrastructure. That's why I believe Plan D should have happened across the rest of the globe. No infrastructure, no Exalls. They can go start from scratch elsewhere."

The Humvee turned sharply, and they found themselves on a straight, undisturbed road that led to Andrews Air Force Base.

"We're here," Ortiz said, brown eyes gazing ahead.

They all looked to find the base demolished, like everything they had passed on the way.

"God dammit!" Camille barked. "I knew it. Knew they wouldn't have left it."

"Relax, Captain," Ortiz replied, raising a hand. "Let's have a look around. This base is massive—there could be a small plane hiding somewhere behind all the debris."

Ortiz swung the Humvee off-road, the regular entrance blocked by the shattered building. They had no obvious way into the actual base, driving around the perimeter of the property for the next couple of minutes. The height of the debris mounds lowered in some spots, providing a glimpse, but there was still no sight of any jets.

"We're wasting time, Major," Camille said. "We really need to hit the road if we're trying to stay on schedule."

They had no set schedule. The mission called for them to sweep major cities and small towns as they made their way to the West Coast. They had budgeted three months for this, but had unlimited freedom to spend their time as they pleased within that timeframe, as long as the job got done. If they wanted to spend two months in D.C. and the final month sprinting across the country, they could. It was normally forty-three hours of driving time from D.C. to San Francisco, but they had no way of knowing if certain parts of the interstate were obstructed or destroyed. Major Ortiz had allocated sixty hours of driving time, leaving them with just under 88 days to spend time in actual cities. They had ten major cities along their route where they would stop, and the initial plan was to spend at least five days in each, covering every mile to search for signs of life. That left thirty-eight days to sweep the small towns in between.

"You're right," Ortiz said, deflated. "We need to be in Pittsburgh tonight, and we have thirteen stops to make before we get there. If we leave now, we should still be able to make it by dinnertime, then we'll get started in the morning."

He flipped the Humvee around and returned to the freeway.

6

Chapter 6

It had been a Thursday like any other three weeks earlier. Robert had woken up with the sun to mow his lawn before heading into the hardware store that he owned and operated in downtown Columbus. He only had maybe four more weeks of cutting the grass with autumn around the corner, shifting his yardwork to raking the blanket of leaves that fell from the two colossal oak trees that watched over his front and back yards.

Robert hopped in the shower and cleaned up for another day at work, heating a breakfast burrito in the microwave before getting behind the wheel of his recently purchased Ford F-150. He had refused to upgrade his old pickup that he'd owned since the early Nineties, but the truck had finally called it a life after racking up nearly 300,000 miles on the odometer.

Gavin, his twenty-five-year-old son, had long been pushing him to join the new century and get a new truck, citing all the fancy bells and whistles that came equipped in any modern vehicle. Robert wasn't one for the glitz and glamours of life, but found he loved XM Radio and the built-in GPS system, using it for every trip, despite knowing his way around town like the back of his hand.

His days at the shop were long but fulfilling. He had always wanted to run his own business, and stepped away from his construction job to do just that after his wife's life insurance check cleared. It was a bittersweet moment, cutting the ribbon on that grand opening, but it was a dream come true. He had named the store after his late wife, Jenny, and decorated the back office with pictures of their many life adventures together.

It had been business as usual: a steady flow of customers in the morning, a dead couple of hours until lunch where he could focus on clerical tasks before the afternoon rush came in. Only on this day, there was no afternoon rush.

The signal that saved his life was a customer who had mentioned multiple cities along the east coast being bombed. Robert pulled up his internet browser in search of news, finding that it was indeed true. Video clips shared from social media showed bombs falling, transforming places like New York City, Washington, D.C. and Miami to piles of ashes within minutes.

His mind kicked into high paranoia, and he tried to piece together what exactly was happening. The news stations were busy speculating on what country was attacking the United States, but Robert knew it was impossible for any foreign entity to have successfully pulled off that many attacks within that brief span of time. It had to be an inside job, and that only meant one thing.

"Plan D," he whispered to himself. Of all the things he had learned from fellow conspiracy theorists, and an anonymous former aide to Bill Clinton, Plan D had been the one thing even he didn't believe. No way the government would, or could, exterminate more than 300 million people living in the country. It was logistically impossible.

But he kept it in the back of his mind. Just in case.

The customer who had nonchalantly informed him of these attacks had strolled out of the store, oblivious that his and hundreds of millions of lives were about to be cut short. But Robert knew, and he wasted no time, locking his shop's doors and speeding back home where his bunker awaited.

During the quick drive, he spotted at least thirty F-16's speed over Columbus, rumbling the world below like an earthquake. The sight of them sent Robert's stomach into a whirlwind, as all the dots were connecting. He had plenty of flashing thoughts where he didn't make it home in time. Surely those jets could circle back within seconds and obliterate the entire city. It was a possibility that always gnawed in the back of his mind. Having the safety of his underground bunker, but being nowhere near when the time called for it.

Robert wasn't one for chaotic driving thanks to a frightening rollover car accident as a teenager. But he gunned the accelerator, touching ninety miles per hour on the side streets, blasting through red lights and stop signs as long as the coast was clear. It all resulted in a record time for his arrival home, when his cell phone buzzed with a call from Gavin flashing on the screen.

"Dad," his son gasped. "Have you seen? It's time. I'm sure you've seen—you're more east than me. I'm so glad I was at home when I saw the first reports. All the main news networks are down, but the local stations are just replaying the videos over and over."

Gavin's words came out as one lengthy, run-on sentence. No pauses for breath, for it seemed as if there was no time for such a trivial task.

"Gav, get to your bunker and wait for it to pass. We know what to do. I just got home from the store and am heading in.

I saw the jets fly over, it's only a matter of minutes until they come back."

Despite his emotions melting into panic during the drive over, having his son on the other end of the phone forced Robert to kick his fear aside, a fatherly instinct that didn't waver with the distance between them. His terror may have bubbled beneath the surface, but he needed to exude confidence after years of building up this very moment.

"No need to worry," Robert continued. "Take care of yourself, and know the world will never be the same after these next few hours. Don't come out until the bombs have stopped for at least two days. Then get to the airport."

"I won't—I swear on Mom."

"No need for that. Try to stay calm." Robert could sense Gavin's panic as if it were pouring out of the phone. "We'll likely have no communication once it hits. I'll come to Denver—get to the airport and I'll be there. I promise. What does the sky look like around you?"

"It was normal, nothing out of the ordinary. This is so fucked up, Dad. Why are we going to be safe while everyone dies? Shouldn't I warn someone?"

The ground around Robert trembled as he started running from his truck toward the bunker, nearly knocking him off his feet.

"No resources for that," he managed to say as the ground shook a little harder. "The jets are back. This is it."

He was only a couple strides from the hatch when the ground trembled and sent him flying toward his finish line. He slid across the grass like a baseball outfielder diving for a ball, keeping his cell phone in a tight grip and immediately snapping it back to his ear. "Are you still there, Gavin?"

Robert looked up to the sight of two dozen jets within a mile, missiles dropping from the sky like a heavy rainstorm. He lifted the hatch and dropped into the bunker, sliding down the ladder and hitting the floor with a heavy thud that shook his knees.

"Gavin?"

"Dad! What's happening?"

"The bombs are falling here. Stick to your plan and I'll come find you. Just stay safe!"

Robert practically spit the words out, knowing time was limited.

The ground rumbled, now above his head, and the unmistakable sound of bombs exploding filled the world above, constant, battering, and deadly. It reminded Robert of the finale of a Fourth of July fireworks show, only more deafening. He felt the explosions rumble in his chest, his body vibrating as if he had been electrocuted.

He kept the phone to his ear, but had no way of hearing. The bunker was made of steel two-feet thick, sure to deflect any missile, assuming it penetrated the additional three feet of soil and grass above its roof. He hadn't turned on any lights, not wanting to tap into his power generator before assessing the final damage above, so he opted to stand in silence below the bunker's hatch, hugging the ladder with his free arm, while the other kept his phone held up.

The barrage of explosions lasted for two consecutive minutes, not so much as a half-second of silence in between. They were bombing Columbus into nothingness—that much he had figured.

His cell phone screen lit up, casting a soft glow across his face, notifying him that the call had ended, flashing a picture of Gavin's young, chiseled face.

"Fuck!"

He tossed the phone aside, where he thought the couch was waiting in the darkness. The cell phone no longer had a purpose. When the bombs finally ceased, Robert only noticed because of a reduction in the noise, but they were still ringing within his head. Even his arms felt like they were still trembling, prompting him to let go of his death grip on the ladder and hold them out in front of his body. His hands were definitely shaking, and he wasn't sure if that was a residual effect from absorbing the vibrations or his own nerves and realization that the world above him was gone. Even for a conspiracy theorist, reality still hit him like an authoritative smack across the face. Suddenly, the dark room spun, and he had no choice but to flail toward the couch on wobbly legs, stumbling like a drunk trying to exit the bar after last call.

He found the couch with his shins, promptly collapsing on to it and leaning back to let his mind and body piece together what the fuck had just happened. Fifteen minutes ago he was in his store on a regular day. Now he might be the only living person remaining in the state of Ohio. The thought made his guts bubble with angst, resulting in an annoying bout of hiccups.

Robert closed his eyes as he lay back, mind rushing with possibilities, flustered that he had survived what sounded like the end of civilization. His body still vibrated, and he realized he was shivering, nerves exploding from head to toe. He wanted desperately to open his hatch and take a look around, but he had to remain disciplined with his plan.

You're safe. Stay that way.

He believed part of Plan D was the possibility of soldiers marching through towns, killing anyone who had survived the attacks.

Those two weeks would certainly be an eternity, but he had equipped the bunker with enough books and puzzles to pass the time, small lanterns to light to preserve the power generator. That could all wait. For now he enjoyed the fact that he was alive, and thought about his late wife as he stared to the pitch-black ceiling, recounting their memories together.

7

Chapter 7

After a long night, the sun finally broke the horizon, waking Kyle and his fellow Crew soldiers. They had arrived to Pittsburgh about an hour before sunset, scrambling to prepare their dinner of canned green beans and bread. Earlier discussion had surrounded whether they would all sleep in the Humvee, or find somewhere suitable.

They came across the grounds of what used to be a golf course just outside of downtown. Minimal rubble scattered around the course, leaving them plenty of options for finding a suitable spot to set up camp. It was a cool night, but not one that required putting up a tent. They wanted to have as few tasks as possible for leaving in the morning, and would only pitch a tent if it appeared rain was in the forecast.

To be safe, they each took two-hour shifts throughout the night to monitor the surroundings. There were still too many unanswered questions for all four of them to sleep at the same time. Safety was the priority in any decision, but the thought of sleeping in the crammed car, breathing the stuffy air all night, led them to sacrifice a couple hours of sleep for the greater good.

They had tasked Kyle with the least desirable shift, standing guard from two to four o'clock, getting to fall back asleep for only two hours until they all needed to wake and begin the day.

He used his time to reflect, enjoying the isolation as the only one awake in the middle of the night, scanning the void of darkness for a threat that surely wasn't coming. As had been the case whenever he had stolen moments to himself, Kyle thought about his parents, praying they both survived the attacks, knowing it was unlikely his mother had succeeded. He thought about Sandra, and what answers she might provide in these uncertain times. Would she have a way of communicating with any surviving Exalls? Doing so could expedite their plans.

He ran through these thoughts over the first hour of his watchdog shift, before realizing this was his first moment alone outside of the underground lair. His three teammates snored behind him, but he focused on the silence that had fallen over the world. No crickets chirping, no owls hooting, no steady white noise of distant traffic. And with no electricity, no ambient light from Pittsburgh, the sky filled with a myriad of stars that appeared on the verge of showering over them, providing enough light for him to see his own hand in front of his face, but not beyond that.

The world had gone dark. Too dark.

Was it really that simple to eliminate society within a matter of hours? Not a single survivor between D.C. and Pittsburgh?

Kyle pondered these matters, a growing sense of responsibility toward restoring society. He and the rest of his team needed to remain loyal to their goals and not succumb to any selfish temptations that might arise—never mind the Exalls or unpredictable humans who may have survived.

Only one Exall mattered, and she hopefully remained safe in her lair beneath Larkwood. Without a doubt, she held captive answers about the current state of the world. Any bit of information had the potential to sway the planet in its next direction. Absurdly enough, even the most man-made massacre recorded still turned into Darwin's theory of natural selection. A whole new level of survival instincts flourished from the added weight of the future's predicament.

The darkness frightened Kyle. It reminded him of the times he'd wandered into his grandmother's basement as a child; the blackness swallowing him whole, truly blinding until he could switch a light on. But in nature, there was no light switch. They had burned a fire until bedtime, putting it out before they all started their sleeping shifts, not wanting the flames to attract any attention.

Staring into the darkness made Kyle feel as small as he'd ever felt. On the other side of the world, the sun was certainly shining. But on what? Was civilization still functioning, in awe of that they had witnessed in the United States? If so, where was the help? Or did the sun rise to greet an equally quiet world? No visitors to the Great Wall, no commotion on the cobblestone streets of Europe. The United States had its history and landmarks, but paled compared to the rest of the world that housed centuries of a past that now may well be forgotten. If there was no recorded history, did it actually happen? Would anyone care?

As he considered this, Kyle wondered if they weren't under as much of a threat as they were from foreign forces. They were a powerful group, the finest secret within the U.S. military. But with no numbers, and no governing force behind them, they essentially stood on land ripe to be stolen. Whether Exalls or another country, their small team had zero chance of fending off an invasion. This grand scheme to cleanse the country of any threats could very well backfire and lead to their death or enslavement.

While this was the darker side of possibilities, Kyle considered what the world might look like if everything went according to plan. Ahead of them waited an obscure opportunity to rebuild the country as they saw fit. They each found themselves in unique positions as modern day founders, each bringing their life experiences, witnessing what had and hadn't worked with their society before the bombs dropped. Kyle was no George Washington, but he could certainly appreciate the fact that no government should have any written plan to make its citizens extinct.

The country had gone dark at one of its most divided times, and now there was no longer a history of the hate and selfishness that had preceded them. Political parties died with the rest of congress. Ideologies now would focus on survival and rebuilding, not on how to put others down to elevate one's self. But there would certainly be outside threats. There always was.

Somewhere in that distant void were Exalls waiting for an opportunity to wipe out any surviving humans. Maybe they were considering options for rebuilding the world in *their* vision. It seemed possible that both the Exalls and humans alike were planning the same things, with different approaches.

Kyle wondered why Plan D had never been revised for modern times. The proposal had been written when Kennedy created the Crew, but it lacked the foresight of knowing what the world would be like today. They should have had plans in place for air transport. Drones would have been helpful to scout the different towns. And if they expected the surviving Crew to rebuild the country, then why the hell was the plan to leave them with virtually no electricity or lines of communication? All that remained were the paved roads and highways, and some stretches of railroad. Otherwise, they were on their own.

Kyle thought of Colonel Griffins, having done so more often since leaving the Pentagon. He had no issues with Major Ortiz, but Colonel Griffins had a unique confidence for any situation that might arise. He wondered what the colonel might have thought about Plan D now that they were living it. Perhaps he had caught a break with that slug in the throat, no longer needing to worry about saving the world. If the Exalls had killed him on purpose, knowing the Crew wouldn't be the same without Griffins around, they certainly removed one of their biggest threats from the equation.

They wouldn't be in any different of a situation at the moment if Griffins had lived, but Kyle would have felt more optimistic for the uncertain weeks ahead. The colonel had been in his role for a couple of decades, working under a handful of administrations and not once losing his grip on the growth and quality of the Crew.

Kyle's thoughts shifted to his grandmother and wondered what life would look like had she survived the attacks in Larkwood. She and Colonel Griffins together would have left no doubt that they would come out of this stronger than ever.

With the countless possibilities swirling around Kyle's mind, he reminded himself that they were at the mercy of the un-known. Tomorrow could bring an uneventful day. Or a threat. Maybe even death. For much of the Crews' existence, they had thrived on taking proactive approaches to their problems. But now, with the fate of the world in its hands, they had shifted to a strictly reactionary approach that left them individually vulnerable, and collectively cautious with every passing minute. Every day, waking up brought a refreshed weight of stress on each of their shoulders, one that would never go away.

8

Chapter 8

The morning remained fairly silent as they all changed into their Crew uniforms. Major Ortiz, having been awake to stand guard at four o'clock, had cooked breakfast over a campfire he created a few feet away from where they slept. He heated a package of sausage and bacon from the stash they had kept in a freezer at the Pentagon, and had since moved to their traveling cooler. They each packed light, squeezing belongings and clothes into small duffel bags, and dedicated the entirety of their trunk space to storing the non-perishable cans of food and three coolers filled with meat to consume over the next week. Prior to leaving, they had a healthy debate about packing containers of gasoline, but eventually decided food and a First-Aid kit were the top priorities. Instead, they packed a tube to siphon gasoline from other vehicles. If it came to it, they would simply move their belongings to another vehicle and keep driving, although they wanted to avoid that, to stay in the comforts of the sturdy military truck.

"We almost ready to head into town?" Major Ortiz called over his shoulder, still rotating the meat he had stuck on a couple of skewers.

"Only if you're making scrambled eggs with that," Bernard replied with a snicker.

"Sure, Lieutenant, coming right up. Would you like a Bloody Mary with that too?"

This drew laughter from Kyle and Camille, who had both been minding their own business as they prepared for the long day ahead.

"I want to leave here in twenty minutes," Ortiz continued, his voice taking on a more serious tone. "I spent my patrol time drawing out a route for us. We should be able to cover at least a third of the city today, hopefully more. I've got us scheduled to hit half the town, understanding we likely won't be able to stop everywhere."

Twenty minutes was plenty of time, and they all scarfed down their preference of pork before packing into the Humvee and leaving the golf course behind. By now, the sun provided full visibility of what used to be Pittsburgh, zero smog in the air, and clear blue skies to contrast the darkness of the night before.

The roar of the engine cut through the silence, echoing all around. They hadn't stopped far from downtown to begin with, and it only took five minutes until they arrived to the scene of a decimated Pittsburgh.

"Everyone hold on," Ortiz said, prompting all eyes to shoot forward for a view out the windshield. Camille rode shotgun and shook her head at the sight of the freeway completely obstructed by debris, piling as high as ten feet in some stretches. Another reason they wanted to keep their Humvee was its unparalleled ability to drive off-road, or in this case, to drive *over* the demolished buildings that once formed the Pittsburgh skyline.

Fortunately, ahead was a small mound of perhaps three feet, a minor challenge for the vehicle, but not impossible. Ortiz crept toward it at a snail's pace, pausing for a brief second before revving the engine and starting their ascent over the Steel City's remains. They all rocked back in their seats, the vehicle at a forty-five degree angle. Rocks and metal crunched beneath them, the sound reminding Kyle of a machine his grandmother used to have that crushed empty soda cans to be recycled.

They gazed toward the crisp, blue sky for a handful of seconds, Ortiz grunting as if he were physically trying to hoist the vehicle over the hill, sighing relief once the front tires dropped on the debris in front of them and started rolling forward again, this time on uneven terrain. Dust kicked up in small clouds behind them, everyone's eyes darting out their respective windows for a complete view of their surroundings.

Downtown Pittsburgh rested inside a peninsula surrounded by three rivers. They had driven in from the southeast where no bridge crossings were required, and it appeared they might have to turn around and head back the way they came to leave the city, as the main bridges in and out of downtown stood collapsed in the distance, only a couple of their towers protruding from the water.

"Eyes up," Ortiz murmured. "I think all of this is from the skyscrapers that used to be downtown. According to the map, we are still a couple miles outside the heart of the city. This area was supposed to be fairly flat, but it seems the debris has spilled all the way over here."

Kyle hadn't been alive during the 9/11 attacks, but he'd seen plenty of the footage on YouTube to understand how buildings spread horizontally upon collapse, becoming a lethal weapon in their own right. Those soldiers tasked with bombing their own country surely had to focus on the skyscrapers. Knocking all of them down took care of half their workload.

"How exactly are we supposed to find survivors out here?" Bernard asked from beside Kyle in the backseat.

"There aren't any survivors," Camille said, nonchalant. "Are you kidding me? I don't think a fly survived this attack. We've already traveled two hundred and fifty miles without a single sign of life. I think their estimates for how many survivors we'll find were way off. The big cities are going to be a waste of time."

"Captain Monroe," Ortiz said sternly. "Please don't undermine our work. Everything about this entire process is absurd and a long shot. Your negativity doesn't help these already trying times."

Camille fell silent, shaking her head before leaning it against the passenger window, banging into it as they hit continuous bumps.

"No negativity here, Major," Bernard said. "But how are we supposed to sift through all this mess to look for people?"

"I'm afraid there won't be much sifting. We're going to have a quick look around different parts that were heavily populated. Otherwise, we should have our eyes set on any structures that may have withstood the bombings—that's where any survivors will probably flock to."

Kyle looked out his window, still shy to question their motives, like the others had done regularly. He didn't understand what they were looking for, either. It was clear no one had survived. The ground itself wasn't even visible, the landscape no different from a massive landfill, scrap metal, steel beams, and broken wood as far as the eyes could see, all topped off with a thick coat of grayish-white ash. As he had done in D.C., Kyle grew nauseous at the thought of them driving over countless dead bodies, possibly even live bodies buried beneath the rubble. Surely out of the nearly two million residents of Pittsburgh, there had to have been at least a couple hundred who had survived but had no way out.

Even if they tried, the four of them couldn't lift the visible rubble enough to free a person, nevermind the potential of risking their own lives if they had to crawl down there for a rescue job. It had grown apparent that a Crew member's life now mattered more than anyone else they might encounter. As gruesome as it sounded, the Crew simply were the only people in the country with any clue about what had happened—and how to move forward. Even one Crew member's death could prove detrimental toward the overall cause.

Only two days back into the world, and it had become clear to Kyle that survival was truly nasty business at its core. Most considered survival an instinct to avoid death, but didn't realize the tough decisions that await at its surface.

"Do you see that up there?" Ortiz asked, nodding straight ahead as his brows drew together.

They all followed his stare to what looked like a standing structure in the far distance, too far to tell for sure.

Instinctively, they all reached for their pistols that never left an arm's reach.

"Simmer down, everyone," Ortiz said. "Probably just some-thing that landed funny and stayed standing. Unlikely a building actually survived. Besides, we still have about a mile and a half until we reach it."

Kyle and Bernard put their guns away, but Camille only tightened her grip and cocked it.

"We don't know what's out there," she said. "Remember, we have no tracking devices. Even if we come across people who appear human, how will we actually know? Did anyone account for that simple fact, or have we already forgotten how the doctor and Kyle's friend roamed the country in human flesh for years?"

Kyle hadn't yet considered this, but she was right. Some Exalls could transform into a human body, but it required an initial consumption of a human's blood. It was entirely possible that a surviving Exall crossed paths with a surviving human and carried out this ritual. But why? Surely any surviving Exall would either want to get the hell off the planet, or shift their focus to rebuilding the land for themselves. The only reason one would need to appear as human was if they thought they might cross paths with other humans—the Crew, in particular.

"That skill is extremely rare, Captain," Ortiz said. "Less than one percent of Exalls had that ability."

Ortiz shot a quick glance into the rear-view mirror, locking eyes with Kyle for a moment before returning his focus to the road ahead.

"All it takes is one, Major," Camille replied. "I believe you taught me that."

"Of course, and you're right. I have no issue with you taking your gun out, just wondering why you did it so soon."

The soldiers fell silent as they continued toward the structure, riding over bumps and hills that bobbed like a shoddy roller coaster. Ortiz had to drive no faster than ten miles per hour on the uneven terrain, taking them a couple of minutes to reach their destination.

"Well, fuck me," Bernard said, his jaw hanging open. "It really is a building that somehow survived. How is that even possible?

They stopped in front of the structure that appeared to be a small doughnut shop. The building had taken a beating, none of the windows surviving, and a sharp crack along the side exterior that caused the roof to lean diagonally. A battered fragment of a neon sign read, "Tasty Donuts", with numerous bulbs smashed and letters missing.

"The only thing that makes sense is if the rubble of all the other destruction somehow shielded this one building, might even be propping it up," Ortiz said, killing the engine. They all stepped out in unison, boots hitting the uneven rubble, causing Kyle to swing his arms to avoid falling. They gathered on the passenger side of the vehicle where Bernard and Camille waited, facing the store.

"We ready?" Bernard asked, cocking his pistol.

"It's what we came to do," Ortiz said. "Let's head in."

9

Chapter 9

Major Ortiz opened the door to the doughnut shop by leaning into it with his shoulder. The door frame had shifted just enough to jam the door, requiring extra force from their muscular major.

"Guns out, but keep them down," Ortiz said after getting the door open. "We're more likely to come across innocent survivors than an Exall."

He entered the building, the other three following. They stood in the entryway, surprised to find the inside of the store mostly untouched. Small piles of debris had formed from the cracked ceiling, and a thin layer of dust covered everything as if it had just gone under construction. But everything else remained. The glass display to the left of the checkout counter housed several dozen doughnuts, and while they still appeared fine and colorful, they were hard as rocks after sitting on the shelves for so long.

"I'll take the one with rainbow sprinkles," Bernard said with a chuckle.

Ortiz shook his head while grinning, puffing out his chest

to shout. "Are there any survivors in here? We are with the United States military. Let your presence be known."

They stood in silence, Kyle holding his breath while they listened for any sort of sound. Nothing ever came, prompting Bernard to sit at a table along the cracked windows.

"Let's sweep the building," Ortiz said. "There could be someone in hiding. Assure them we're here to help." He spoke these words, confident they would come across another human life. Kyle wasn't sure why he had given up hope already—this was only their second big city, first where they actually got out of the vehicle to search.

The doughnuts lined up with the left wall and connected to the counter that housed the cash register. A hallway between the counter and the next wall led to the bathrooms and a back office.

"Franzen and Wells, check the restrooms," Ortiz commanded.

Kyle suddenly became dizzy, swaying on his legs as the room spun around him. He felt like he could faint on the spot, but leaned against a table for balance, not showing his temporary lapse of weakness in front of his fellow soldiers. The kitchen tugged at him.

Bernard stood up and started toward the bathrooms. "C'mon, Wells."

Ortiz and Camille waited in the lobby, both inspecting the area.

"Would you hide in a bathroom?" Bernard asked Kyle over his shoulder. "Seems an obvious hiding spot to me—not very effective."

Kyle only chuckled, still fighting to regain his composure. Bernard stopped in front of the two restroom doors, looking to both the women's and the men's as if it were a critical choice on which to open first. He stuck out a wavering hand to the women's door on the left, grabbing the shiny knob and twisting.

He flung the door open and shrieked immediately, jumping back and bumping into Kyle, sending him off balance. Ortiz and Camille promptly cocked their guns and sprinted around the corner to meet them.

"Oh my God!" Bernard cried out, a slight giggle clinging to each word. "It was a rat." He panted for breath as they all looked into the bathroom and saw the rodent scurry away, a quarter of a doughnut clutched in its mouth.

"Are you kidding me, Franzen?" Ortiz snapped.

"I'm sorry, Major," he replied. "Guess I'm a little on edge."

Everyone broke into a chorus of laughter, Bernard even dropping his hands to his knees to hold himself up. They fought off the laughter over the next minute, eventually settling back to normal when Bernard stepped into the restroom.

The bathroom had two stalls, and he looked underneath both, confirming no one was hiding. Kyle went into the men's room and did the same.

"Nothing," Kyle said as he rejoined the group, now huddled.

"Let's check out the kitchen and office," Ortiz said, pivoting away. "If there's any rats back there making doughnuts, show yourself, or Franzen will shoot!"

This drew another round of laughter, Bernard shaking his head as he slipped his pistol back into his utility belt. "I guarantee any of you would have had the same reaction, but of course it had to happen to good ol' Bernard."

"You didn't even shoot the rat," Kyle said. "What a waste!"

Ortiz chuckled as he raised his hand. "Let's relax. We can tease Franzen for the rest of this trip, but let's focus on getting out of here."

He nodded for Camille to join him as they headed toward the kitchen. Camille hadn't put her gun down since they stepped out of the truck, as if she *wanted* something to happen.

"Kitchen is clear," Ortiz said over his shoulder after ducking to see below the industrial ovens. "We have a door—looks like for a small office. Heading in now."

Ortiz stopped, freezing before his fingers reached the door-knob.

"What's wrong?" Camille whispered, sensing a sudden shift in the major's mood.

"I think someone's in there."

He stepped aside to let Camille view the frosted glass window that only allowed them to see a darkened silhouette, completely still.

"You think they're alive?" she asked.

Ortiz shrugged. "It's only been a few seconds, but they're not moving."

He pulled out his pistol and cocked it.

"They're either dead, or waiting for us," Camille said. "We've definitely made our presence known."

Ortiz waved over for Bernard and Kyle to join them, nodding toward the office door. "We may have something," he whispered.

They cocked their necks for a better view and promptly drew their guns. "We got your back," Bernard said, nodding for Ortiz to open the door.

Ortiz nodded back before returning his attention to the door, shouting. "If you're in there and hear us, let yourself be known or we may shoot you."

All eyes focused on the silhouette, watching it remain completely still. Ortiz shoved the door open, whipping his pistol ahead of him.

The door banged open against the wall, revealing a grinning Exall seated behind the desk.

"Oh, look!" the Exall cried. "The little humans have come to kill me!"

"Don't move!" Ortiz shouted back, both hands on his pistol aimed at the gray-skinned alien.

They pointed all guns at the Exall. In fact, everyone's breathing kicked up another notch at the sight of an imminent threat. With Ortiz leading the group and being closest to the Exall, they awaited his next move.

"Why are you sitting in here?" Ortiz asked, lowering his voice, but keeping it authoritative.

"The question is, why did you destroy this beautiful planet, Mr. Ortiz?" the Exall asked, leaning back and crossing its arms, eyes reading the name stitched into the major's uniform.

"We didn't," Ortiz said, finger tightening on the trigger.

"We found it very strange that you would decide to do this. Killing your own people because you're afraid of us?"

Now play along with me, Major, and let's have some fun, the Exall's voice said within Ortiz's head.

"Get out!" Ortiz barked, each word requiring him to muster all of his energy. "Get out now!"

The three soldiers exchanged glances, not following what their leader was saying. Did he really want the Exall to just walk out of the front door? The Exall stared at him, not speaking a word, but maintaining a curious gaze.

Turn that gun around, Mr. Ortiz, and take out your little group. We can have so much more fun, you and I.

"No!" Ortiz screamed. "Stop it! Get out!"

Ortiz clenched the gun so tight it made his arm tremble. A sensation spread up his back, filling his arms and fingertips. It felt as if someone had cast an invisible lasso around his wrist, fighting to tug the pistol in the other direction. He fought, gritting his teeth as he kept the gun aimed at the Exall, sweat forming around his forehead.

Camille had seen enough and took a stern step forward to blast a choker bullet square between the Exall's eyes. Its head kicked back, the tarry, black blood splashing on the wall behind like a spilled bottle of ink.

Ortiz gasped for breath like he had just run a marathon.

"He was taking over your mind, Major," Camille sneered. "You know the protocol for when that happens. Why didn't you give us the sign?"

If a Crew member ever found themselves in a situation of having their mind hijacked, the code toward their peers was three kicks on the ground with a heel. Ortiz hung his head and shook it.

"I had absolutely no control," he said. "It was like being put in a chokehold from behind, totally blindsided. It felt like hands around my throat... I had to fight to even speak. How did you know?"

"It's something that always fascinated me, and I've just kept studying how their mind control works. You showed all the symptoms—shouting nonsense, body stiffening, avoiding eye contact with your peers. Besides, I'm not sure why you were conversing with the bastard anyway—should've blasted him right away."

"I know that, and I won't make that mistake again. I guess I just had my hopes up too high that it was going to be a human. Maybe someone taking a nap. I honestly didn't think we'd encounter Exalls so soon, and in such a large city."

They had all known Major Ortiz as a man of sound reasoning and practicality, always viewing situations from all angles. He had never been caught off guard until now, and because of that, no one held it against him.

"You've been preaching it all along, Major," Bernard said. "The world is unpredictable now. We have no way of knowing what to expect."

"More importantly," Ortiz added. "We just saw the importance of sticking together as a team—all four of us. If Monroe wasn't here, what would've happened?"

"He would have made you turn your gun on us," Camille replied. "And either kill us all, or convert us into Exalls."

The comment sent chills down Kyle's spine, the reality hitting too close to home.

"Well, thank you for knowing what to do," Ortiz said.

"Let's get out of here," Camille said with a nod. "Clearly no humans to rescue and lots more ground to cover."

10

Chapter 10

Travis Wells ate the last remnants from his cans of green beans and peaches, enjoying the combo for a celebratory Sunday night dinner after surviving another week in his underground bunker—well, his mother's bunker. She had instilled in his mind since he was a teenager to restock the bunker every eighteen months.

So he did just that, marking the calendar in his phone to remind every year and a half to take out the old cans, drop them off at a homeless shelter, and replace them with newer cans. Everything else in the bunker was taken care of: the cases of bottled water, a gas-powered stove, and even the makeshift toilet with plumbing that supposedly connected to the main sewage line.

It was a routine he had to reacquaint himself with after his mother was taken away, but one he jumped back into without missing a beat. The thought always crept into the back of his mind, pondering why he was still going through such a silly process every other year. Was it paranoia? Nostalgia? Perhaps a way to stay spiritually connected with his late mother?

He didn't know, and wasn't one to set aside the time to think of such things, but as he lay on the small cot in the bunker, was glad he had kept at it. He could survive an entire year, and if the world wasn't safe enough to step outside by then, what was the point of living further? His mother had been thoughtful enough to leave calendars all the way through the year 2090, along with a pencil to cross off the days as they passed.

Travis had been in this bunker for twenty-four days and had already completed many attempts to break out. The hatch above was jammed, not budging a centimeter despite the force of his thrusting shoulder. He was trapped, but didn't panic. He had once been explained the process of Plan D, and knew he had a three-month window for the Crew to make their way across the country and check all the known Crew-built bunkers.

Travis spent his days exercising—running in circles, followed by crunches and push-ups, fearful of gaining weight from doing nothing all day. His mother had only left behind romance novels, so he had no choice but to become familiar with the works of Nora Roberts and Danielle Steele. He'd grown to like the books, but would deny touching them if asked.

Not having any technology proved difficult at first, but he adapted after a week. Travis rather enjoyed the peace. No news to watch, no sports games to kill time, no cell phone buzzing all day with its incessant flow of seemingly irrelevant alerts. He had time back, and even though he was trapped in a room with survival resources, wanted nothing more than to evaluate his life and figure how to make it more fulfilling after escaping this hell.

With the world gone, what would life look like? Would the Crew try to recruit him? Out of all the citizens who may have survived, he surely had the most knowledge of the Crew.

Besides, his mother had been a major figure and influence within the organization. And who knew what kind of name Kyle was carving out for himself in his early days. Travis might have no option but to become an official member and dedicate the rest of his life to restoring the country.

He'd deal with that if the time came. For now, he needed to strategize any other possible ways out. He had caught a brief glimpse as the bombs dropped, the monitors underground flickering to life with different camera angles around the property, but once the house crumpled under the bombs, the feed cut away. The camera installed on the garage had provided a view of the house just as it collapsed.

"It's only wood and siding!" he had cried out after his shoulder turned sore from ramming it into the hatch hundreds of times over the last few weeks. Twice he budged it, dust falling through the cracks, but it was never enough to actually open the door.

Giving up, Travis shifted his focus to rummaging through the file cabinets that housed notes from his mother. Surely there had to be a tip somewhere in the wealth of paperwork that suggested a way out should the door be barricaded, but then again, it was a small room with no obvious exit. Instead, he found notes about the Exalls—dry reading compared to the stack of romance books at his disposal. Even though the content was dull, he still enjoyed flipping through the notes, most of it handwritten by his mother. He'd catch himself brushing his fingers over the grooves on the paper, ink fading in some spots after being written nearly fifty years ago.

At one point he had cried, his tears splotching the ink and turning the paper crusty after drying. The cabinets strictly contained information about the Exalls and Crew. Travis had hoped he might come across old family artifacts, but never did. This left him with nothing but distant memories that ranged from childhood all the way through his adult life.

The underground bunker was never a secret for Travis, and he was taught at six how to access and use it, just in case his mother wasn't home and tragedy struck. Every three months, Susan ran through drills with him, leaving him to reach the bunker in as fast of a time as he could. It was a sport to her, Travis her young track star who needed to do better than his previous recorded time. She pushed him, sometimes threw in obstacles, but he never wavered, developing an instinct to reach the bunker quickly and efficiently. These days of drills always ended with dinner at a restaurant, followed by a stop at Mr. Scoop's Ice Cream Shop on the way home.

At his young age, Travis never understood the seriousness of what he was being taught. He was just a kid doing as his mother asked. It wasn't until high school when she sat him down at the kitchen table and had a long, thorough discussion about what exactly she did for work, where she was always traveling, and that he couldn't tell a soul about any of it. Unless he wanted to risk being silenced by the United States government.

Travis knew how badly his mother had wanted him to grow into a Crew soldier, but gave up on that dream when he couldn't replicate the same excitement for such a lifestyle. He always wondered why she never had a direct conversation with him about the matter, instead dropping subtle hints and tests to gauge his abilities. These mind games reached their peak during his high school years and promptly faded once Travis went to college in Boulder. It wasn't until many years later, when Kyle was seven years old, that Travis recognized his mother pulling the same experiments on her grandson.

He had never drawn the parallel before, but now realized his own son had been forced into the same situation. Even worse, Kyle had come face to face with the Exalls at twelve years old, only to join the Crew after his seventeenth birthday.

Regarding Kyle, she had sat down with Travis for a lengthy conversation about the boy's future.

"I know you can't see it," she had said. "But Kyle is very gifted. Enough that we need to make sure his future always points toward joining the Crew. Can you make that happen?"

"I'll do what I can," Travis had replied, knowing damn well the fight that awaited with his wife, Lori. It had indeed turned into one of the biggest fights of their marriage, but Lori eventually agreed to go along with it after some additional convincing from Susan. Their agreement boiled down to a soft guidance toward the Crew. If Kyle showed interest in a different career path, they wouldn't discourage him, but wouldn't encourage him, either. Should he ask about the military, then they would break out their full support behind that decision and do everything to help.

They had expected a struggle in achieving this, but the whole plan was thrown out the window when the Exalls attacked Kyle's middle school. The family secret leaked, Travis and Lori divorced, and the Exalls took Susan's dead body away. All within a three-week window that threw Kyle's life into limbo.

Travis often looked back to that moment in their lives as the grand turning point. From that time on, their family had broken and everyone essentially went their own ways, forging their own paths as individuals instead of as a fully functioning unit.

And now it all led to this. Lori was dead. At least, he assumed as much. She would have been at work with no way of knowing what was coming. Kyle was hopefully alive and on his way. And that left Travis alone in the bunker, surviving, clinging to his will to live, praying that the rescue team would indeed make it to Larkwood in time.

11

Chapter 11

"I have a major secret to share," Kyle said as they cruised along I-70, going 95 miles per hour a couple hours outside of Columbus, Ohio. They had left Pittsburgh with no further excitement, minus a pile of dead bodies they found under rubble after hearing what they thought were cries for help. It ended up being a stray cat, a couple of scratches across its face, but otherwise in sturdy shape. They quivered at the thought of the cat gnawing on all those corpses as it clung to survival.

"Ooh, a secret!" Bernard cried from the backseat. They had maintained a rotation of where they sat in the car, and it was finally Kyle's turn to ride shotgun. Major Ortiz insisted on driving once again, not having taken a break from the task during the entirety of their venture that was now on day six. "This should be good. Is it about your crush back home? Were you going to propose?"

Kyle furrowed his brow and grinned at the same time. "What are you talking about?"

Bernard cackled, the only one laughing in the car. "I don't know, just trying to guess what kind of secret an eighteen-year-old kid could have during times like these."

"Don't act like you don't have skeletons in your closet," Camille said to Bernard. "We've all got things we can talk about, and I'm sure it's only a matter of time until we do. We're about to be together for an absurd amount of time."

"We'll give you some space once we get into a groove," Ortiz said. "Pittsburgh was hectic, being our first stop. Dayton is your hometown. So perhaps after that things can somewhat settle down."

Camille wasn't just the only woman on the squad, she was the lone introvert. Six days with no alone time was already taking its toll and put her into a more somber mood than usual. No one else had any issue being trapped in a car for days at a time with each other, but Camille might consider an offer to ride in the trunk if it presented itself. Anything to get away.

"Are you going to tell us or tease us?" Ortiz asked.

Kyle drew a deep breath, elevating the tension in the vehicle without realizing it. Everyone fell silent in anticipation of something new to break the continuity their lives had become on the road.

"I don't know if I should say it yet, but it has to do with what's waiting in Denver. I need you all to believe me and trust that I know what I'm doing."

"I doubt any of us are going to find anything we want back at home," Bernard said. "Did you see Pittsburgh?"

"What I have is still there. It's underground and perfectly safe. We'll have to get to it, might have to dig through all the debris, but it will be worth it."

"Just tell us—you're building this up for disappointment," Bernard said, smacking the back of Kyle's seat.

"There's a living Exall underneath my grandma's house."

He said it, and there was no turning back. His heart raced, the world swirling around him as he awaited a response from the only people on the planet who could appreciate the news.

No one responded right away, the only sound that of the humming engine as they continued to tear down the freeway. Kyle's words hung in the air like a rain cloud. He kept his head forward, but glanced out the side of his eye to Major Ortiz.

Ortiz maintained his focus on driving, but Kyle saw the swarm of millions of thoughts buzzing around his head like flies around an open dumpster.

"Nah," Bernard said. "No way that's real."

"Hold on," Ortiz said, raising a hand. "Is this true, Wells? You've seen this Exall for yourself?"

"Of course. I found a whole secret laboratory connected to my grandma's bunker. She left hidden notes for me as clues. She knew I'd be in the Crew one day—really weird stuff."

"Does it speak?" Ortiz asked, his face scrunched into a studious expression while keeping his focus on the road. "What kind of studies have been done? Is it constrained? Why hasn't it tried to break free?"

"Her name is Sandra. My grandma rescued her after an attack and brought her to her house. She strapped her to a table in that lab. Says she won't harm us—she feels indebted to my grandma. I barely met her for the first time for a few minutes before I got called back to D.C. That was the day before the big battle, so I obviously haven't been back since."

"There's no way," Bernard said. "We've been trying to capture a live Exall for so long. It's never happened. And we're supposed to believe that one soldier pulled it off by herself?"

"If he's saying it, why don't you believe him?" Camille snapped. "Why does everything have to be a fight with you?"

"Whoa! Calm down there. I'm just trying to make sense of it all. Of course I know Wells isn't making it up for shits and giggles. This is absolutely major news."

"Did your grandma leave you any instructions about what to do with her?" Camille asked, as if they were discussing a baking recipe rather than a living, breathing extraterrestrial.

"I'm sure she did—there were even more files in the lab, but I didn't get to look through much of it."

"You're certain the lab will have survived these bombs?" Ortiz asked.

"Yes, it's beneath her basement, deep enough that it shouldn't even be affected."

"And is it possible your dad will stumble across this little secret?"

Kyle shrugged. "I suppose it is, but there is a hidden eye scanner to open the secret door. I guess it's a matter of whether my grandma scanned my dad's eyes to have access—which I don't believe to be true."

"Jesus Christ, Wells," Camille said. "And you've known about this since Plan D started?"

He nodded. "I had told Colonel Griffins about it right before they shot him. When that happened, I didn't know what to do. It's been this huge secret just eating at me this whole time. I've wanted to tell you guys since day one, but didn't want to add any extra pressure for us to get out. . . and I didn't know how well I could trust you all."

"If you're in the Crew, you're family," Bernard said, using his most serious tone. "There's no bond more sacred than living this secret life. Every single Crew member you meet has had to sacrifice all their normalcy, their safety, their friends and family. I've never met someone, since joining, that I've felt I couldn't trust in the slightest. We would all lay our lives down for each other if it came to it."

"I know that now, after spending those three weeks underground with you all. This has just been such a heavy secret. I don't even know what we're really working with because I didn't have enough time to look through all those file cabinets of notes. This can be used for good or bad, help us or hurt us—we don't know. I was afraid of the Crew just storming into my grandma's house and taking Sandra away without an explanation... or worse."

"I can't speak on behalf of what Colonel Griffins would have done," Ortiz said. "But the way I run things, it's up to you. What do *you* think we need to do about this?"

The response caught Kyle off guard and made him shift in his seat.

"I—I don't know. We should probably take it slow and not do anything rash out of emotion. We need to read through all the notes to get a full understanding."

"This is going to add some time to our stay in Denver," Ortiz said. "How long do you think it would take for all of us to split up the notes and read through them?"

Kyle shrugged. "I'm not even sure how many notes there are. I only saw the file cabinets and don't know if they were all full. If we assume they are, I think we should be able to read through everything over the course of a full day."

"Not bad."

"Maybe, but we don't know what we'll have to do after," Bernard said. "Surely we're not going to leave a live Exall and continue to California. But, we don't exactly have the space to let an Exall ride with us. Unless we tie her up and cram her in the trunk."

"Or on the roof," Camille added.

"This is what I was afraid of," Kyle said, instantly feeling attacked. "There's no need for us to be mean to her. She posed no threat, and I was standing right in front of her. Didn't even suggest she had any ill will toward me. We have no right to hurt her unless we need to."

"Once an Exall, always an Exall," Camille said. "I won't trust any of them for a single second. I don't care what they say, what the notes say—we must remain vigilant. I wouldn't be surprised if this was a long game they've been playing. Since when do the Exalls let one of their own remain hostage by humans? Never in my time in the Crew have I heard of such a thing. It's a trap."

"She's been kept hidden," Kyle said. "Impossible to reach. Even when the Exalls were in my grandma's house, they didn't make a move for the basement. I think they legitimately had no way of knowing Sandra was down there."

"Unless Sandra is the one pulling the strings," Major Ortiz said. "While I don't think it's likely, it's a possibility that we need to keep in mind. Hopefully Mrs. Wells has in her notes what abilities this Exall has. If this one has mental abilities, there's no way of knowing for sure what game they're trying to play. If it could enter your grandma's mind without her knowing, it could have been leaking our intel to fellow Exalls across the world."

"Then why would they kill my grandma?" Kyle asked. "If they had a direct line of communication with an insider like that?"

"I don't think they killed her," the major replied. "It's been debated. And sure, her tracking device went dark, but that doesn't mean anything, especially if they took her off of this planet. There's basically two trains of thought. Either they killed her because she posed one of the biggest threats to them. Or they took her hoping to pick her mind and gain all the possible information from her. This theory lines up more with what we know of the Exalls, and neither has been debunked so far. But if they just wanted her dead, why take her body?"

"I watched her on live video from her bunker," Kyle said, tears welling in his eyes. "She was shot in the back and bled. Collapsed. It's pretty clear she died."

"I understand that. Everyone in positions of power has viewed the video. The thing is, we've never had an instance of Exalls taking a dead body. Not once. And there have been plenty of Crew members killed in the line of battle, but they always left those bodies behind. Until Susan. That's *why* there's a debate."

"It's true," Camille said. "Every single Crew member that an Exall has ever killed has had their bodies recovered. Except for one."

Kyle had heard none of this before, the data gnawing at his stomach as he thought of his grandmother potentially alive. Floating in space? On a spacecraft? Possibly even still on Earth, hidden in a remote location?

"Thank you for letting me know—I didn't have a clue. I suppose this changes how we should approach Sandra. At least I know to not trust her so easily. But I still think our priority needs to be going through the notes."

"I agree, and that's where we'll start," Ortiz said. "But for now, I need you all to try to not think about this so much. We can't afford to lose focus on the task in front of us. We'll be stopping in a little over an hour and can't have any more surprises like we did in Pittsburgh."

That much was true, but the thought of a living Exall under

these circumstances would press on all of their minds until they eventually arrived in Denver.

72

12

Chapter 12

It only took a week for Robert to venture outside of his underground bunker. The silence convinced him it was safe enough. There had been no vehicles, no voices searching for survivors. Besides, he had gradually grown more paranoid that his bunker's hatch had become covered with debris. He needed to know sooner than later if this whole thing had backfired, leaving him to die in the bunker's privacy where no one would ever hear his screams for help.

Just another forgotten life in the grand scheme of things, he thought. This pushed him to open the bunker to see what had become of the world. The mental games had exhausted what had been a rather logical mind when he headed in. Even though he was only a couple days away from sitting on his front lawn to pass the time, his thoughts at the moment had transformed into ones of doom and despair. He feared for his son every second of the day and had to find a way to Denver as soon as possible. They didn't have time to wait.

With two pistols tucked in his waistband, and a stomach full of canned beets, Robert climbed up the short ladder to his hatch and turned the dial on the combination lock that he had custom set to 06-23-02. He had married his late wife on June 23rd at two o'clock on a sunny afternoon.

Entering the combination caused a brief flash of heartache, knowing this whole thing would've been easier to cope with had she still been alive. Then again, her death and the following spiral into conspiracies is the reason he had a bunker to begin with. Even in death, she kept him alive.

"I love you, Jen," he said, pulling the handle that opened the hatch, sunlight immediately spilling in and blinding him after seven days in dimness. Not a day had gone by since her death where he didn't feel her presence, standing right beside him for eternity, as they had vowed.

He rose all the way out of the bunker, fresh air filling his lungs, but not with the usual crispness he expected. Instead, death and a gray haze filled the air. The blue skies above were still somewhat visible, but it was like he had a pair of light sunglasses over his eyes. He looked around at the sight of demolition and despair. His house was flattened, along with every other home in the neighborhood. There were a couple of homes that remained partially standing, perhaps one wall, but no more. Most cars had been flipped, some remained flat on their tires with plenty of damage done to their exteriors. Power lines tangled around the mounds of debris like a spider's web.

"Jesus Christ," Robert whispered under his breath, the world spinning around him. He always knew Plan D was bad, but had never fully grasped its severity until this moment. Patches of the road were visible, weaving in and out of the various mounds that had formed across the landscape. "I've gotta get out of here."

He scanned the area for any vehicles that appeared to be in

one piece, but did not immediately find anything. He had some experience with mechanical work, so if he could even find a car that needed repair, he should be able to restore it back to functionality. Denver was over one thousand miles away, and without knowing how many gas stations remained standing between here and there, he'd have to plan to either drive as far as possible on a tank of gas and switch vehicles in another town, or find somewhere to stock up on any excess gasoline for his journey. Fuel-efficient cars, though he hated them, would be his best chance. He would only need about three full tanks of gas to reach Denver. Or if he could find a semi-truck, that would be better than striking gold, particularly if it had a full tank. If that was the case, he'd be able to make it all the way to Colorado.

There simply wasn't anything available for Robert to choose from his immediate surroundings. He'd enter town where there was certainly a higher concentration of civilization, and a better chance at finding something useful.

He took a moment to settle his racing mind, dragging himself to the pile of wood that was once his house, and had a moment of silence—pure silence in the new, quiet world. The memories rushed him, suffocated him as he lost his will to live. It was the first and only house that he and Jenny had lived in after getting married. It's where they raised Gavin. Birthday parties, backyard barbecues, and all of their friends and family over for holidays only scratched the surface of images playing back in his mind.

He had taught Gavin how to throw a baseball on this very yard, ran alongside him in the street when first learning to ride a bike, and feeling that heavy mixture of pride and despair when his only son finally took off on his own and rode around the block, out of sight. Tears welled in his eyes, and he hadn't even yet thought of all the memories he had with his beloved Jenny. They had shared plenty of weekend mornings tending to their garden of flowers, only to find the days give way to nights where they sipped beers around a fire pit in the backyard, reminiscing on their life together, looking forward to Gavin's bright future.

The emotions grew too strong, causing Robert to kneel and let the tears freely flow. He didn't mind being alone, had become used to it ever since his wife had passed, but there was something different about not being able to look out the window and see civilization. He had no window. No civilization. He was as alone as one could be, an eerie sensation as he glanced around, destruction his only companion.

"It's okay," he whispered to himself, the same words echoing from several years in the past when his wife had been killed. Pastor Jones had uttered these words, embracing Robert at the funeral, moments before all the friends and family showed up.

"Life is a never-ending cycle of challenges," Pastor Jones had continued. "Some are harder than others—some unbearable—but we must never stop growing and learning from these. With every death comes new life. With darkness comes a new sunrise. It will take time to realize these truths, but that doesn't make them any less true."

Robert had clung to these words, the pain in his soul never waning, but his mind able to focus on other things. In the months following the burial of his precious Jenny, Robert experienced how every day felt like a fresh start. His routine and daily life had been uprooted, his slate cleaned. He had wanted nothing to change, but soon needed to roll with the punches, or risk spending his days crying in the basement as he sifted through boxes of old memories.

It wasn't much longer afterward for his idea to open a new hardware store in town—he had quickly grown tired of having to drive almost thirty minutes across Columbus to support the only family-owned business within a fifty-mile radius. He hated the big-box stores and had no issue making the trip, but the thought had soon planted in his mind to open his own and let that be the focus of his new life as a widower.

After a year of looking at different properties, filing appropriate paperwork with the city and state, he opened Jenny's Hardware and Tools, crying at the end of a long, successful opening day. He became a staple in the community, getting to know most families, and certainly all the contractors who worked around town. Robert never had an urge to date another woman, instead deciding to carry on his wife's legacy through the store.

It became his home away from home, his emotional haven. While the house contained all of their memories, the store was fresh and kept her spirit alive. He could morph the business exactly as he wished, conversing with the two pictures of Jenny that hung in the back office, as if her final stamp of approval overlooked every decision.

I need to get to the store, Robert thought, suddenly consumed with that as his only goal. He didn't expect a different scene at the shop, but felt he needed to at least stop by and see what remained.

Walking would take him about thirty minutes, so he started immediately, leaving his home behind without another thought. It had quickly become apparent that no other person was going to magically pop out of the ground like he had, but he kept his pistol in his waistband, just in case he came across any of the secret government members who had authorized this apocalyptic scene.

He trudged through the gaps of open space he could find, occasionally climbing small hills of the neighborhood's remnants. He had known nearly everyone that lived on his block by first name, calling out said names as he passed each property, just in case anyone survived the brutal attacks. The only voice that called back was his own, each time sending a wave of gooseflesh across his neck and back.

It only took five minutes for him to realize that Columbus was now, somehow, his town. And another five minutes before the cramps started working their way from his stomach into his thighs and calves.

I'm way too old for this shit.

At 62 years of age, he had pondered plenty of times over the past week if this was all even worth it for him. It wasn't a matter of what he had to offer—he still had plenty in the tank. But was it worth it to live another twenty years if the next fifteen, at least, were going to be dedicated to rebuilding the country, and possibly the world? And what did he have to fight for in the twilight of his life?

Robert toyed with these thoughts and various scenarios as he continued walking. If he encountered one of these secret government workers—or worse, an Exall—would he run for survival, or stand there and let them take his life? He couldn't truthfully answer that question for himself, and supposed the decision would come down to the reality of it actually happening.

For now, all he could do was keep his head down and his feet moving forward.

13

Chapter 13

When Robert reached what remained of his store, he broke down into sobs. His store was completely gone, as if it had never stood on its ground for the last decade. No sign, no crumbled walls, not even a lone hammer from the hundreds he kept in stock. It was like someone had come in the middle of the night and literally erased Columbus from the map. While he expected to find destruction, the complete nothingness caught him off guard, and somehow it was more silent than at his home.

He had hoped to salvage the store sign, or on the off chance, the photos of Jenny, but he quickly realized the walk over had been a waste of time, leaving him to peruse the area for signs of *anything* that resembled the town that once stood here.

Just as he would do in his neighborhood when he returned, Robert called out for the names of the other business owners who called this strip mall home. Over the years he had be-friended not just the owners, but plenty of the regular staff members from the coffee shop, ice cream parlor, and the pizza joint. They'd bring him goodies, and he always lent them any tools they might need for repairs in their shops. They were a family for Robert, even if they didn't all realize it.

The ghosts of these colleagues didn't haunt him as he marched through the deserted town. He had no more emotional capacity to weep, not yet. He called out the names he knew, confident and emotionless despite a tinge of fear creeping up his back. The loneliness really wrapped its grip around his throat once he was in downtown. After ten minutes of aimless wandering through the debris, he decided it was best to just turn back and head home. At least there he had the security of his own property, not to mention the stockpile of food and weapons.

He heard what sounded like a distant motor, causing Robert to spin around in search of the source, locking his sights on what was indeed a moving vehicle. His heart froze in his chest, and he dropped to the ground to crawl out of sight, sliding beneath a thin sheet of metal protruding from the ground just enough for him to fit.

With his heart pounding in his ears, he reminded himself that there were only three possibilities should he encounter life: an Exall, a government member, or a layman like himself.

Thirty-three percent chance they're just like me, he thought, shaking off the idea. It only made sense, at this early point in time, for it to be the government. Who else would have access to a vehicle unless they knew to fully prepare for what had happened?

I'm the conspiracy theorist who was correct. I'll be damned if the government erases me like they did the rest of the country.

Unfortunately, the conspiracy ended where it began for Robert. He had gained his knowledge of Plan D from an anonymous tip on an online message board—someone who had claimed to work closely with Bill Clinton. But he still had no idea what the plan was for the aftermath. Perhaps the government *wanted* to find survivors. Or maybe they were driving around to kill anyone who lived. It could even be survival of the fittest, every man for themselves. In that case, they could lay eyes on Robert and simply keep driving by, leaving him to scrap for whatever remained of his life.

"This is all so fucked up," Robert whispered to himself, wanting to hear his voice to ensure he was still alive. It had even crossed his mind that he had indeed died in the attacks, and this was all some sort of twisted purgatory on Earth.

But the hollowness in his chest felt real, the salt in his tears strong as they streamed around his lips. And the musty stench of death that lingered in the air as if it had been there for hundreds of years.

The engine grew louder and closer, and Robert fought to keep himself completely still, despite knowing that anyone inside the loud vehicle wouldn't hear him breathing. He curled into the fetal position, holding his knees to help stay still.

It could have been ten seconds or ten minutes that passed until the truck approached him, the sound of its tires crunching over the road of debris. He didn't bother trying to get a look at exactly how close they were, but he estimated it was at least within fifty feet, close enough for the smell of exhaust to slip into his senses.

The engine stopped, the world falling back to silence except for Robert's heart drumming, trying to leap out of his throat. Doors opened and closed, followed by footsteps hitting the ground. The blood froze in Robert's veins as he had a sudden panic attack, terrified that his life would now end with him balled up like a coward under sheet metal.

Dear God, please don't let it end like this. Make them get back in their truck and leave. Robert hadn't prayed since the bombs dropped, his Christian faith shaken to its core. But now he begged to God, and couldn't help but feel a tinge a guilt for this being his first dialogue with the man upstairs.

"Anyone out there?" a woman's voice called out, authoritative. Multiple whistles rang out, echoing, as if they were all searching for a lost dog. "If anyone is alive out there, please let your presence be known!"

The woman shouted, her words showering over Robert's trembling body. Footsteps crunched around, seeming to go in different directions.

It's over. They're going to find you and put a slug in your head.

He didn't know if his best play would be to reveal himself, or try to remain hidden. It depended on the people's motives—which he had no way of knowing. He wished he had positioned himself with a view of them, then he could make a better informed decision. Did the people have guns? Medical kits? Both? Revealing himself was the only way to know for sure, but he couldn't bring himself to do it, his legs frozen stiff with adrenaline.

Footsteps approached closer, walking right up to the other side of the sheet metal, prompting him to hold his breath for complete silence. The feet stopped, and he heard the breathing from whoever was standing mere inches from him. All they had to do was walk around the sheet metal and he'd be found.

Play dead, he thought, doubting he could hold his breath long enough without his face turning red. But it might be his only option if he heard them approach any closer.

"I got nothing, Captain!" a man's deep voice boomed from above Robert, making him flinch. The feet crunched as they pivoted and started back toward the vehicle. Robert let out a long sigh of relief as he listened to the voices convene. They weren't talking loud enough for him to make out the conversation.

They conversed for five minutes, and Robert worried they would make another round, but they finally gave up and returned to the truck, the doors slamming, providing the most refreshing sound he had ever heard. The engine fired back up and they were on their way, leaving as abruptly as they had arrived. The motor moved away from Robert, allowing him to wiggle his way out of the crevice that had protected him, peeking to see them continue westbound.

I'm going to follow them, he thought. *As soon as I find a vehicle.*

He didn't know what sort of pace they would travel, but figured if they were moving west, I-70 was their best, if not only, option. He, too, needed to use I-70 to get to Denver, and this just might be the excuse to get him to leave behind the security of his home and hit the road. There was no hurry, though. Robert didn't *need* to know where these people were going or what their business was. Simply knowing they existed and were in the vicinity was plenty of information. He'd hang low for the next day or two, just in case they planned to hang out in Columbus any longer. Even if they somehow found him on his property, they'd have no way of entering his bunker, it's only lock being from the inside.

He grinned once the truck was out of sight, spinning around to head back home, knowing the road ahead would be filled with plenty of excitement. The simple trip he had planned to Denver now became more complicated with the addition of these government folks, but he'd have no issue dodging them—especially if he was trailing them from behind. He only wished there was a way to let Gavin know they were out there.

14

Chapter 14

They arrived in Dayton by mid-afternoon, the sun hiding behind an opaque rain cloud. "Soak it in," Major Ortiz advised as he weaved through debris to stay on flat road. "Welcome to the hometown of our very own Captain Monroe. What can you tell us about growing up here?"

Camille sighed as she shook her head, eyes glued outside the window where memories passed her by. "It was tough growing up here. We didn't settle in Dayton until my dad retired from the Marines when I was going into sixth grade. We lived in one of the more affluent neighborhoods. I was only one of three Black girls in middle school, and one of seven in high school. It's already hard jumping into a new town at that age when everyone already has their circle of friends... It was even harder being so different from everyone else."

"Were you bullied?" Kyle asked.

"Not bullied—at least not in the active way you might be thinking. Kids were friendly and polite to my face, but they rarely invited me to parties or events outside of school. I eventually fell in with a small circle of two other friends. We always felt the eyes staring at us, almost like we were lepers that no one wanted to approach. It really was a nice town, I just felt that I could have had a better experience."

"Sorry you had to go through that," Bernard said. "People can be so gross."

"It's fine. I have no regrets about growing up here—it's where my life is rooted and now that I'm back, it's sort of relieving, even with everything gone."

"What are we looking for here?" Bernard asked. "Anything special?"

"I need to see if my parents made it. I had a bunker set up in their basement—just like I'm sure we've all done for our parents—but they were always doubtful they would need it. Last I heard, they had a heavy dresser blocking the bunker door." Camille chuckled, shaking her head. "I've had plenty of arguments with them about it, and made them promise to clear the way. No idea if they ever did, but I guess we'll find out soon enough."

Her voice cracked, and Kyle turned around in his seat to find that her eyes had filled with tears. He had yet to see such raw emotion from his closed-off captain, but gained even more respect for her by witnessing her vulnerability. Military members had tough façades to maintain, and the Crew seemed to have it even worse. Conversations around family and life back home were rare, and when they came up, often sounded like a historical recounting instead of someone's actual past.

"It'll be fine," Bernard said, reaching over and patting Camille on the knee.

"We gotta stop in the heart of town," Ortiz said. "Then you can direct me to your house."

Anticipation suddenly grew thick within the truck. While they each had something they wanted to check in their hometowns, this was the first instance of someone in the squad encountering their demons. They didn't know what to expect, aside from another city being a mere pile of ashes. But beneath those ashes were memories close to Camille. She'd already shown more emotion than she ever had. What would happen when she saw her childhood home obliterated? How would she react if her parents hadn't survived, inches from the bunker that they dismissed as over-the-top paranoia?

Ortiz stopped the truck a couple minutes later, killing the engine.

"This is downtown," Camille said. "I spent my first two years at community college here before I went to Columbus. My first apartment, my first full-time job, it was all within this two-mile radius. I walked everywhere and loved that freedom—still miss it to this day."

Her voice shook but never cracked, and they all knew this trip down Memory Lane was only going to intensify the closer they got to her parents' house.

"I've never been to Ohio," Bernard added for color commentary. "I always wanted to go to a Buckeyes game, but never had the chance."

This earned a grin from Camille. "They were as fun as they looked on TV—better, of course. I suppose it's only my word to say that we were the best school and football team in the world."

Bernard nodded as he smiled, glad to have lifted her spirits, even for a moment.

"I don't see anything worth scouting here," Ortiz said, keeping them focused. "Not too many skyscrapers in town, Captain?"

"Nothing special, a couple of tall buildings, but none to write home about."

"I figured as much—it's pretty flat here. I'll keep driving around and see if we find anything notable. Which direction is your parents' house?"

"Southeast."

"Got it."

Ortiz fired the engine back up and continued driving at a slow, steady pace, enough for everyone to gaze out their windows for what they had since dubbed "hot zones"—areas of elevated debris that suggested a cluster of buildings had existed, increasing their chances of finding potential survivors.

This mission of surveying the desecrated cities would only last a few more days. If there were any humans trapped beneath rubble, they would only live between one to three weeks without food and water. If any had access to water, or even a generous rainfall, they could survive beyond a month with no food. Plan D was already three weeks behind them, shrinking their window of opportunity for trapped survivors.

"I got nothing on my side," Kyle said, his eyes dancing around the bleak landscape. It reminded him of a massive landfill stretching as far as his vision allowed.

Everyone else in the vehicle had the same results, prompting Ortiz to take them southeast, leaving downtown behind. Kyle felt Camille's leg bouncing on the seat behind him, sparking an anxiety within himself that he hadn't expected until they reached the Colorado border.

"Just tell me the way, Captain," Ortiz said, picking up the pace a bit.

"Keep going, it's about five minutes on this road—or at least it used to be."

Now it felt like a rumbling on Kyle's seat, like those electronic massage chairs he'd used in the malls for his twenty-second sample. The landscape never changed. A couple mounds protruded from debris, prompting Ortiz to drive slowly around them with the windows down, calling out for any potential life. Only his voice echoed back. The reality had settled in that they would find no one. So far there had been one Exall encounter during their entire time since leaving D.C., not quite the recipe for the successful rebuild they hoped for.

Camille guided them through an area that was even flatter, clearly the remnants of a neighborhood with one-level homes. Their drive across the country had allowed them this new skill of judging what had once stood on the destroyed ground they drove on.

"There it is!" Camille snapped, pointing ahead. A splotch of bright red stuck out from the ground, looking like a blood splatter at first. The bunkers were designed to deploy a red flag if their surface ever became disturbed, the sole purpose to help identify where the bunker lay among a landscape of wreckage, another fine detail foreseen by the Crew. No one in the car had ever seen it in action until now. "Oh, thank God!"

Ortiz sped toward the flag, the Humvee rising and falling as it drove over the neighborhood. He came to a stop ten feet away, everyone jumping out of the vehicle without hesitation, following Camille as she led the way to the flag, squatting down to pick it up and yanking on the rope attached to it.

The rope tightened, sending dust and shards of wood into the air, clearing a path toward the bunker. The flag dangled below Camille's tight grip, flapping with each tug as she gritted her teeth, looking like a body builder attempting to pull a semi-truck in one of those absurd competitions.

The men wasted no time once they realized a sheet of siding was the culprit causing the restraint, hustling over to it and each lifting a side to throw it out of the way, revealing more rope.

"How long are these things?" Kyle asked, one of the minor details covered in his Crew education that had easily slipped his memory.

"They fire about forty feet into the air," Major Ortiz said. "They're shot out like an airbag in a car. But even though the flag is a thick fabric, they can't travel much higher than that."

They each grabbed a part of the rope, now appearing like a team ready to dominate a tug-of-war contest. Roughly thirty feet of rope was visible, and they pulled to shake off more of the rubble, Bernard shuffling toward the front to kick aside more wood and what appeared to be melted chunks of roofing shingles.

After three more tugs—accompanied by hearty grunts from everyone involved—the end of the rope became visible, tied to a thick steel hook that had been welded to the top of the bunker.

"We got it!" Bernard cried out.

The bunkers were designed to have two entrances, one from the top, and another from the side, positioned inside the home for easy access. They all started brushing away the debris piled atop the bunker, dusting aside a clear path to the hatch, a keypad visible that Camille immediately lunged to and started punching in the combination that she had set up many years ago.

The hatch popped, Camille grabbing it and nearly throwing it to the sky. "Mom! Dad!" she gasped, swinging her legs into the bunker, sliding down the ladder like a firefighter. Her boots hit the ground below, and she immediately shrieked. The men above gathered around the open hatch, looking down, Camille sitting against the wall opposite her parents. They sat leaning back against the wall, hunched in toward each other, hands clasped and eyes closed. Motionless.

"No, no, no, no," Camille whined, her hands visibly shaking.

"We'll be right down," Major Ortiz called, turning his attention to Bernard. "I need you to stay up here. Always good to have someone outside in case something happens while we're down there."

"Yes, sir," Bernard said, no way of lightening this mood.

"Wells, come with me."

Kyle nodded and followed behind Ortiz, who started down the ladder. He had a brief flashback to jumping down his grandmother's bunker, wondering why she didn't have a full-length ladder installed for an easier descent.

When Kyle reached the bottom, Ortiz was already squatting in front of Camille, running his hands up and down her arms for what little emotional comfort she could receive. Kyle had hoped that maybe Camille's parents were just napping. But it was clear they had been dead for a few days. He spotted a white envelope resting beside her father's limp hand.

"There's a letter," Kyle said. "Should I grab it?"

He immediately regretted offering, realizing he had never voluntarily approached a dead body. Sure, Colonel Griffins had died in his arms, but that was a chaotic sequence of events.

This situation, however, was an obviously dead body that he now needed to walk right up to after Camille nodded. Fortunately, the envelope lay on the ground, not clutched in the man's hand where Kyle would have had to encounter his fears in a more direct manner. He shuffled over, unaware he was holding his breath as his body tensed. He gave thanks that both of the bodies' eyes were closed. Had they been open in their mindless, distant gaze, Kyle may have let his breakfast go all over the bunker floor.

He bent down and grabbed the envelope, a brief whiff of the corpse filling his nose, stale and pungent. Kyle's head spun when he stood back up, part of his mind expecting the dead man's arm to reach out and grab him. Surely that wouldn't happen, though, because there was no such thing as zombies.

Just like there's no such thing as aliens.

He spun and returned to Camille and Major Ortiz, who hadn't moved from their positions.

"Will you read it, Major?" Camille asked, her wet eyes gazing up to their leader. "I would try, but I know I won't make it past the first line."

"Of course. It'd be my honor."

Kyle slid the envelope into Ortiz's grasp and was glad to be done with the situation for a moment.

Ortiz cleared his throat as he thumbed open the envelope, pulling out a handwritten letter on lined, loose-leaf paper. "Cam, we want you to know that we always believed what you told us about the bunker, even if it didn't seem like it. It was hard for us at first, but we soon realized you had no reason to lie or exaggerate the reasons for needing this. Thank you for thinking of us and opting to save our lives when so many others won't have that opportunity.

"We are proud of you. From the moment you were born, you have filled our lives with countless blessings. We always had high hopes for you and never imagined you would surpass what we always envisioned for your life. You are a hero. You are selfless. You are caring and kind. Never lose sight of those traits and you'll always be okay in this world.

"We're sorry you had to find us this way. This is not how we imagined the end of our lives would look. We were watching the news when the random attacks started on the east coast. Your father pieced it together and understood what was happening. We were scared, but brave, thanks to you. We only caught a glimpse of the world before the television feeds cut out. The world is now a place where survival is the lone priority every day. That is not a world either of us wanted to live in.

"Please don't think this was a rushed decision. We're writing this letter after three days together down here. Three full, complete days of discussion, prayer, reminiscing, and crying. We reflected on the life we built together and decided we have nothing further to achieve. We're too old to worry about surviving. We've already fought our fights and wouldn't dream of hindering whatever comes next for this world. We wanted a peaceful death, and we plan to overdose on some pain pills. They say it's a rather painless way to go, and that's all we want.

"Don't let our decision change anything about your life. Keep fighting your battles. We'll always be watching over you, and we can't wait to see you again someday. We love you. Mom and Dad."

Major Ortiz folded the letter and stuck it back in the envelope.

Camille had sat silently throughout the reading of the letter, but tears streamed in every direction, making her entire face shine from the eyes down. She sniffled and cleared her throat. "I can't believe . . . this is what I came home to. I can't believe they used the bunker to do this. For years, they made fun of the bunker." She stopped and bit her trembling bottom lip, shaking her head. "I need a drink."

"You'll have a drink as soon as we find one, Captain," Ortiz said, standing back up and crossing his arms. "I know it's not a question you were ready for, but what do you want to do with your parents' bodies?"

Camille patted the tears on her cheeks, throwing her head back and bonking it against the wall, something that didn't appear to faze her. She shrugged. "There's not exactly anywhere to bury bodies right now—I'd like to leave them here."

Ortiz extended his hands, dropping them in front of Camille's face. She took a few more seconds to gather herself before grabbing the hands and standing up. Ortiz didn't need to say it, but she knew they were in no position to spend any more time in this bunker than they needed. With no lives to preserve, they had made a vow before stepping foot outside of D.C. that they needed to keep moving forward.

Without another word, Camille forced herself to her parents and planted a kiss on each of their foreheads, patting their hands that remained held together, their souls intertwined for eternity. Fresh tears poured from her eyes, but she turned and started back up the ladder, Ortiz and Kyle following behind.

15

Chapter 15

It took a couple of hours, but Robert restored a lightly damaged Ford Focus he had come across while walking back home. It was a drastic change from his old pickup truck, a vehicle that he insisted a man like himself would never drive. But it was the end of the world, and he had no other choice.

He giggled after the engine revved, the sound closer to a dying cat than a roaring lion as he had grown accustomed to, and loved. There was no vibration when he sat behind the wheel, the interior cramped as he felt the need to crouch, his knees practically touching his ears as his legs were too long for the tiny car. He offered a quick prayer of thanks for finding the vehicle, now enabling him to start his trek to Colorado, but also prayed to find a new means of transportation once hitting the road. The thought of traveling 1,200 miles in this thing made his stomach flip.

The government vehicle was long gone, but he still planned to wait another day before hitting the road. He wanted to follow them, but not too closely, and not knowing their planned stops caused him to play it extra safe. They needed to be in his sight, not the other way around. It was a straight path to Denver from Columbus, but if Robert ever sensed he was being followed, he had no issue swerving off the freeway and taking an alternative route.

For now, he had to plan how to best pack this sad excuse of a vehicle for ultimate success on the road. The trip should take two days of driving at least nine hours each day. That sounded right for his current physical shape, and being able to break those nine hours into two separate chunks would still leave him with plenty of time for a full night's sleep.

The thought of hitting the road gave him a new wave of energy, and he moved with urgency once he arrived home, heading straight into the bunker to take inventory and measure what all would fit into the trunk, backseat, and passenger seat of the Focus. He had months worth of non-perishable foods, but sitting around for half a year simply wasn't an option, especially knowing the government insiders were out there roaming around.

Robert moved cans of fruit and vegetables to the bottom of the ladder, along with cases of water. He had lost a step since his younger days, and knew it would take a physical toll on his body to make multiple trips up and down the ladder, carrying the supplies. But he had no choice, and even though the car was small, it would still house hundreds of cans and water bottles.

The task seemed daunting, and he thought of having to transfer all the supplies to a new vehicle when the time came.

"I'm not getting to Denver in two days," he said to himself, shaking his head as he ran back and forth from the base of the ladder to the pantry.

It took him just north of forty minutes to pile everything he estimated would fit in the car against the wall next to the ladder.

Sweat dripped down his back, making his t-shirt cling to his skin. He stood with his hands on his waist, taking quick gasps for air as he looked over the small mountain of water and food. It hardly made a dent in his overall supply, maybe twenty-five percent of his total inventory.

"Planned for six months of survival," he said aloud, shaking his head. "Only to pack a month's worth into a tiny hippie car."

Next was the daunting task of lugging all of this stuff up the ladder. But first he needed a moment to gather himself and regain some strength. His mouth watered at the thought of a juicy steak and ice cold beer for a relaxing meal, but there was no steak, and the beer was only cool thanks to being stored underground.

Deflated once again by the reality surrounding him, Robert dragged himself up the ladder and returned to the car to pull it right up to the bunker's hatch. He popped the trunk open and froze when he thought he heard a voice in the distance.

He held his breath and didn't move a muscle, senses heightened as he concentrated entirely on the surrounding sounds.

Maybe it was the wind. Something fell over. It could have been anything.

Only it couldn't be *anything*, considering there was *nothing* to begin with. He thought back and didn't recall feeling so much as a light breeze since coming out of the bunker. The sun rose and set each day with no other significant weather, a detail that now seemed more chilling as he thought about it.

Robert didn't have time to dwell on that, and would have to revisit the thought later. For now, he thought he heard a snicker, again in the distance. Hearing actually became difficult as his heart reverberated within his ears like an obscure drum.

"It could just be a cat, running through all the mess and

knocking shit over." He spoke these words out loud to both break the tension that had consumed his body, and snap out of the mental trance he had fallen into.

A cat—or any stray animal—seemed a logical conclusion. Just because he hadn't yet encountered any didn't mean they weren't out there in the vast demolition. Surely some creature had survived and was now clawing its way out. Hell, even a mouse could jump on something at just the right angle and cause a domino effect of other things to topple over.

Robert shook his head, wary of believing such a simple explanation, preparing for something worse. He turned and started back down the hatch, the shotgun in the back closet on his mind.

Even with a tired body, his legs pumped anxiously toward the closet in the far back. Nothing was locked within the bunker, so he swung the closet door open to reveal a rack holding four hunting rifles, four AR-15's, and ten handguns along the bottom base. Boxes of ammunition stacked in neat towers along the sides, a bulletproof vest resting from the middle hook. After stocking the bunker with food, the armory was the next priority, and he spared no expense, knowing all means of survival would one day be fair game.

Robert grinned as he grabbed a shotgun, confirming it was indeed loaded, as every other firearm should have been. He returned to the hatch and climbed up the ladder with a renewed sense of energy. The fear from before had given way to a determination to encounter whatever waited in the distance. If it was anything besides an alien, he liked his chances. And even if it was some creature from another world, he still felt positive, knowing he'd remain within a quick dash of the bunker.

When he reached the top and stepped foot on soil, a gentle

breeze blew over, ruffling his hair, and making him laugh at himself for his paranoia earlier. "Of course there's been wind," he said. *Just been too distracted to notice.*

Robert drew his focus back to the sounds in the area, the world silent as it had been. He debated shouting, just to see if anything would respond, but decided to remain hidden as best he could. He wanted to be the eyes watching whatever might lurk from the debris, not the other way around. His breathing finally steadied for the first time in several minutes, making his hearing even sharper.

That's when he heard something, this time a growl of sorts. It reminded him of when their old dog, Biscuit, an energetic golden retriever, would try to play tug-o-war with his chew toy, Robert howling laughter as he held on for dear life. But Biscuit always growled like it was his final task to complete in life, hellbent on getting that chew toy back in his sole possession.

The sound carried from roughly four houses down, the old Foster residence. Nothing remained on their lot except for a bent pole with a basketball backboard attached, its rim nowhere in sight. Their house had been just as flattened as Robert's, but he was certain that's where the sound was coming from and started taking slow steps in that direction.

The noise convinced him it was an animal, so he found no harm in looking. If he was lucky, maybe he'd find a stray dog that would become his companion in this lonely world—God knows he needed *something* to keep him company. If not, he'd let the critter continue on its path and quest for survival, just like him.

He stepped silently, practically tiptoeing, as he made his way toward the sound. A few mounds of debris protruded from the otherwise flat landscape, and Robert assumed the animal was taking its sweet time behind its protection. He stepped on a patch of gravel that seemed to echo around the entire city, prompting him to freeze in his spot and draw his ears to focus on the sound he was chasing. The growling continued uninterrupted, so Robert moved forward, keeping a closer eye on the steps in front of him.

When he reached the outer edge of what used to be the Fosters' property, his grip tightened on the shotgun, the growling much louder, crisper, and clearly belonging to that of a dog. Robert drew a deep breath, suddenly paranoid the dog could be rabid. Anything seemed possible in this now dismal world.

Don't be such a pussy, he told himself. *Even if it's a rabid* bear, *you're still the one with a gun. Rabies ain't invincibility—they still drop with a bullet to the head.*

He chuckled at the thought of a bear roaming the streets, cocking the shotgun, just in case. Robert stepped around chunks of concrete that he believed would crumble more if stepped on, now close enough to distract the creature. The unmistakable sound of flesh being ripped off bone filled the silent airwaves, churning Robert's stomach with disgust. Sweat trickled down his back and arms, slickening his grip on the shotgun. The day had been hot, but it seemed someone had cranked the temperature up a few notches.

You're just nervous.

He pinpointed precisely which mound the noise was coming from behind, eyes narrowing on it as he inched closer, finger sliding over the trigger.

Robert took a deep breath before taking the final steps around the hill of debris. At first he saw nothing, momentarily puzzling him, but then he saw the pair of black shoes protruding from the ground, caked with mud. The feet connected with legs that disappeared into the debris.

It's a person? Robert thought, his mind unable to make sense of what his eyes were seeing. Now he debated turning and running, but he still wasn't sure what was eating what. There could have been a dog underneath the rubble, chewing up what surely would have been Mr. Foster. Or was it some other person wandering through town who ate a dog—or a corpse. Surely the couple of weeks that had passed weren't enough to turn someone into such a savage so soon.

If he left, it didn't seem he'd be followed, and he'd be able to plan for handling a cannibal on the loose. Or he could stay and address the situation with a swift pull of the trigger.

"No chickenshits out here," he said under his breath, clearing his throat. Even doing that didn't divert the attention from the man or animal. The feet hadn't moved for the entire minute he'd been standing there, so he thought it was indeed a corpse being further mutilated from beneath.

"Hey!" Robert shouted, and the feet promptly kicked back and spun around, arms, hands, and the rest of its body appearing, all the way up to a gray face. "What the fuck?"

It wasn't Mr. Foster, not even close. The face had no familiarity, and Robert tried to look beyond the gray skin, assuming this person had caught some sort of disease. Between the man's teeth was a limp, dangling forearm, the flesh tattered, blood oozing from his lips. He stared at Robert, eyes blank and dark, as he opened his jaw to let the severed arm fall to the ground.

Robert had his shot lined up without even realizing it, and squeezed the trigger. The slug caught the gray man square in the chest and sent him tumbling back. Adrenaline kicked in for

Robert, and he spun around to run back to his house. He had walked over to chat with Mr. Foster on several occasions, the quick trip feeling like a quick thirty seconds each time. Now, however, the distance back to his house never seemed so far, but he pumped his legs like his life depended on it.

He stole a quick glance over his shoulder and saw the man rise back to his feet and start chasing after him. He didn't appear to be running anywhere near Robert's speed, but the world was also passing by in a blur, all sense of time and space completely jaded. Robert's vision couldn't keep its focus, pulsing in and out as he dashed for the bunker.

His heart pounded, lungs gasping for air, as he hadn't sprinted in at least forty years. He checked one more time to ensure the man hadn't gained on him, relieved when he saw him the same distance away. It only took him forty seconds to reach the bunker, but he practically jumped into it, slamming the hatch shut and turning the wheel to lock it. He stumbled through the bunker, intoxicated with adrenaline, dropping the shotgun next to the couch before making his way to the back room, where he raided the closet for all the guns and ammo he could hold. A couple of boxes of ammunition fell to the ground as his hands trembled. Robert returned to the base of the ladder and dropped the weapons on the ground.

His legs were on the verge of giving out, even with his body calming itself. No matter how hard he tried, he couldn't erase the image of that limp arm hanging from the man's mouth, his skin sickly, eyes petrifying.

"That was it," Robert panted. "That was the fucking alien—had to be."

He had no plans on taking another gamble to find out for sure. The next time he left the bunker would be to finish loading the car and get the hell out of town. His pile of guns now took a higher priority over food—he wouldn't dare get caught unprepared again.

16

Chapter 16

Camille hadn't spoken a word since they left Dayton two days ago. The entire squad had little to say, a cloud of depression hanging over all of them. Major Ortiz had told Kyle, during their overnight stay in Cincinnati, that after enough years with the Crew, many members grew a bond closer than family. Ortiz and Camille had long worked together well before these new squads had formed, so he shared her pain. Kyle and Bernard were the odd men out, certainly feeling horrible for Camille, but not quite on the level of understanding. She needed her time to mourn, and with these circumstances of virtually no privacy, they expected the process to take longer than normal.

Kyle had tried connecting on an emotional level with Camille, telling the story of how he witnessed his grandmother get slaughtered by the Exalls. They had sat around the campfire, but she only tucked her chin into her knees, letting tears stream down her face. He had made his effort, and understood nothing anyone said would be enough to pull her out of the doldrums—she'd have to do that on her own.

The slight buzz and excitement that had accompanied them

on the first leg of the trip had completely vanished the moment they left Dayton, and they could only hope it would return at some point. For now, the mission felt like plain old work. Bernard still had his father to check on in St. Louis, and the scene they had left behind at Camille's childhood home left a sour taste in all of their mouths. It forced Bernard to face his own pessimism regarding what awaited a few hours away, and no one could offer him any words of support. Not after what they had all seen.

Cincinnati saw them go through the motions, checking likely locations for any signs of life, knowing damn well the most important thing they needed to do was get to Denver to check on Sandra. They still had to go through Louisville and Indianapolis before starting their journey to St. Louis. Major Ortiz didn't have to say it, but witnessing his friend's sudden sadness took a toll on him. He grew short and demanding with his orders, sometimes apologizing afterward, sometimes not.

Anxiety engulfed their entire squad, the mission having originally started as a well-planned itinerary, now an uncertain sequence of potential chaos. They were only a quarter of the way across the country and had already encountered an Exall and two dead parents. The road ahead no longer showed much promise, the future along with it.

They were now on the road to Louisville. The car ride remained silent, but Major Ortiz finally spoke up, unleashing the thoughts that he had bottled up since they left Dayton.

"What do you all think of hurrying this trip?" He let the question hang, knowing it would catch everyone off guard.

"How do you mean?" Bernard asked after a few more seconds of silence.

"I mean getting to Denver feels urgent now. I don't know

how in tune you all are with your gut feelings, but mine are telling me we have to find that Exall and see what she knows. At the very least, what Susan's notes can tell us. We've been traveling through all these cities, and outside of the encounter in Pittsburgh, we've come across absolutely nothing."

"So you want to just head straight to Denver? Blast through all the other stops?"

Kyle sunk into his seat as Bernard questioned the major, the reality of returning to his hometown and encountering Sandra now thrust to the top of Ortiz's priorities.

"Not at all. We'll still stick to our route, but I'm thinking we no longer need to set up camp and do these extensive walkthroughs of each city. Every location has looked exactly the same. There are no survivors out there. Who are we kidding?"

"I've thought that from the beginning, Major," Bernard said. "The big cities are a waste of time. They designed the attacks to hit the big buildings and let their collapse cause the damage. We should spend our time looking in rural areas—God knows there's been plenty of it."

"I've been keeping an eye out while we drive past farms and the random houses or stores we've seen in the distance."

"Sure, but that's not gonna do anything. Any survivor isn't going to wave their arms to get our attention. They're already used to being remote—this has only made them want to stay inside for fear of their life. If they see a car coming, they probably run for their tornado shelters for protection. We don't have an actual way of finding these people unless they want to be found. It's too out of the way to stop at each one, all for the possibility that no one is even home. Look there, for example."

Bernard pointed out his window to a large barn in the distance, the vast fields deserted, yellowing both from the autumn and lack of attention over the past couple of weeks. No animals were visible, all machinery stagnant. A windmill twirled in slow motion, capturing the little momentum offered by the soft breeze.

"We'll probably pass hundreds of these between here and Denver," Bernard said. "Perhaps it makes more sense to stop at a few of those instead of driving through big cities."

Ortiz nodded, his eyes fixated on the road ahead. "We could—I still don't think that's a useful way to spend our time."

"Isn't the point of this trip to find survivors to repopulate the country? We need to find someone."

"That's the long-term goal, yes. Though, we need to ensure the country is safe before taking that next leap. No point in having babies and pregnant women if we're running from Exalls. We need to ensure they no longer exist."

Those words cut Kyle in the gut. Did that mean Sandra had no chance of surviving? Now he wondered if it was a mistake telling them what awaited in Denver.

Just let them meet her and decide for themselves, he thought, knowing even from a brief encounter that Sandra was the least threatening Exall who ever existed. But he knew that didn't matter, and that it would come down to what Sandra could provide the Crew in terms of help. If proven beneficial, they'd certainly keep her around, but if she posed so much as a minuscule threat, she might as well be signing her death warrant.

It was personal for Kyle. He wasn't attached to Sandra by any means, but he felt she was his grandmother's most significant project, clearly the biggest secret of her career, and the last living part of her legacy. Sandra had to be preserved for these reasons, and he'd do everything within his power to make sure that happened.

"For what it's worth," Kyle spoke up from the backseat. "I think we should get to Denver soon. We know Exalls can sense each other's presence. Sandra will be just that for us—a radar. A real life tracking device."

"I've been thinking the same thing," Ortiz said. "Not only that, but if she can communicate with other Exalls *and* is legitimately on our side, we can use that to set traps and ambushes. That's something we've only dreamed about." The major chuckled and shook his head. "I'll be damned."

"What is it?" Bernard asked, looking around as if expecting a sight outside the vehicle.

"Susan Wells was known for having a high amount of ambushes on Exalls. It all makes sense now. There's no way for anyone to set up an ambush like that. Multiple times are impossible. I think this Exall in Denver is our key to everything."

They fell silent for a few seconds, letting this idea marinate. Bernard spoke first. "It makes sense, and I don't doubt it, but I can't help but feel a need to resist. What if this was the Exalls' long game? Did they always see this moment coming, ready to unleash Sandra at the last moment? A sort of checkmate with the world already in shambles."

"We can't rule anything out," Ortiz replied. "That scenario seems unlikely, but still possible. Why would they wait for us to destroy ourselves? They have always enjoyed harming humans, why wouldn't they be the ones to deliver the final blow?"

"*This* would be the final blow. Don't forget how smart and advanced they are. We don't know for sure, but can only assume humanity has them outnumbered. They caused so much chaos to the point of making our government kill its own population—just pulled the plug on society and made us disappear like we were never here. Did the Exalls know this would be the result? We have no way of knowing, but they have been inside the Pentagon, they've hijacked our people's minds. Whether or not they knew doesn't matter, what they were waiting for was an opportunity. Maybe our decision just handed them the world on a silver platter. I've always questioned the reasoning behind Plan D, and I suppose we'll find out soon enough if it works or not."

"No conspiracy theories," Ortiz snapped. "This isn't the place or the organization to spew that nonsense."

Ortiz was too loyal to the Crew to entertain a thought as wild as Exalls playing a long game like this. Other theories that circulated the secret military branch included one that the Exalls started the Crew, either by hijacking President Kennedy's mind or someone in his administration. They set up the Crew as a machine to execute Plan D one day, chipping away toward it every three decades until now, landing in a time so divisive and tumultuous that they could push it through. They believed Plan D was, in fact, the work of the Exalls to fulfill their lifelong goal of overruling Earth.

Kyle had learned some of these theories while going through his early training—they even directly mentioned them in some of his lessons, promptly shooting them down with a string of facts explaining why such a theory couldn't be true. But isn't that what an organization would do to steer their own members away from such a disturbing reality? He had thought little of it until now and couldn't help but wonder. On the surface, the theory made sense, but wasn't that the point?

"The Exall in Pittsburgh went down too easy," Kyle said. "That has to debunk the theory—it didn't even really try fighting us. And why would they sacrifice one of their own in such a meaningless way? Surely if they had orchestrated this entire thing, they wouldn't waste a second to further play games."

"Thank you," Ortiz said, nodding in agreement. "It's been three weeks since the country has been demolished, and we've encountered but one Exall. If their plan was to invade and populate the world, we'd have seen more by now."

Bernard grumbled something under his breath as he held his gaze out the windshield.

"I'm telling you," Kyle said. "Sandra had a calming, gentle presence. I really believe she has no negative intentions toward us. I think my grandma showed her over all these years that we can be trusted. Maybe *she* was the one playing the long game—so long that she knew she wouldn't even be here to see it play out. The ball's in our court with Sandra. We need to go through all the notes and find out what our next play is."

"This is exactly what I'm thinking," Ortiz said, grinning with joy that someone was speaking the same language. "That's why we're going to Denver as fast as we can."

17

Chapter 17

Once Camille finally spoke up and agreed that getting to Denver was their top priority, all of their originally scheduled plans changed. Major Ortiz had driven them into Indianapolis, arriving around dinner time, where they stopped to chow down a few bites from the assortment of canned foods stored in the trunk. They ate and stretched their legs for about ten minutes before hopping back in and driving around the city for an hour.

From there, Major Ortiz let someone else drive for the first time on the trip, swapping spots with Bernard in the passenger seat. Bernard took them back onto the freeway toward his hometown of St. Louis. Denver was twelve hours from St. Louis, and Ortiz opted to skip nights camping out and stay on the road, creating a rotation that allowed two of them to sleep, while one drove and the other remained awake as a co-pilot.

Four hours separated Indianapolis and St. Louis in normal times, but Bernard made it in just under three, blasting down the freeway without a care in the world. He had volunteered to take the driving shift, knowing his excitement to arrive home would push any fatigue aside. Fortunately, the freeways remained completely clear in the rural areas. They only encountered blockages near the bigger cities where much of the rubble toppled onto the road and made them take different routes to enter and exit.

"I can't believe it," Bernard said, shaking his head when they arrived shortly before midnight.

"What's wrong?" Kyle asked, having volunteered to stay awake with Bernard.

"I knew the city would be gone just like all the other ones we've seen, but when it's your hometown, the place you grew up watching out of the backseat window, it's just sick and wrong. I'm sure you'll know what I mean when we get to Denver." He pointed ahead, eyes bulging. "Over there was the Gateway Arch, and behind it was the rest of the city skyline. Some of the most beautiful sunsets in the world, and I don't just say that because it's where I'm from."

"I don't know, I think Denver could give you guys a run for your money. We had the sunset over the mountains and the city in front. I've never seen that anywhere else."

Kyle gave Bernard a nudge across the center console, suddenly nauseous after realizing he had just spoken of Denver in the past tense, subconsciously confirming his hometown was also a pile of ashes.

"I'm sure the mountains are a sight to see, but the arch, the river, the city . . . it was just something else. There's not a lot of beauty like it in this part of the country, and we had it right in the middle of America. Our views were a source of pride, and we had such a diverse range of people living in and around the city. Everyone respected each other. Everyone had such a blue-collar approach to life. No place like St. Louie."

"You think your dad is okay?" Kyle asked, his tone more

serious. Since they were close enough for Bernard to point out where certain landmarks used to stand, he figured they were at least within a half hour of arriving at their destination.

Bernard shrugged. "I don't think he did anything like Camille's parents, but it's just a matter of him being home or not when the attacks started. If he was home and sensed the danger, I know he's in the bunker. But my dad also enjoyed going on walks in the park, visiting friends, spending hours at the library. It's a coin toss, honestly."

"I'm in the same boat," Kyle said. "Obviously my dad has known about the Crew for nearly his entire life, but if he wasn't home, then I guess there's nothing we can do about that."

Bernard nodded. "I've already come to terms with the likelihood that my dad won't be there. I figured if I set myself up for that, then I can only be surprised if he is actually alive. My gut tells me he's really gone, though."

"I'm sorry, man. This is all so surreal still—I can't believe these are things we're having to deal with."

"It's part of the job, I suppose. We all know going in that you may not make it out. We also know that our families might not make it out either, depending how much they decide to talk. I guess the end of the road is the same for all of us in the Crew, no matter what we do with our careers."

"Do you think Plan D was always destined to happen?"

"I don't think so. Keep in mind that they designed Plan D to be the last resort. I don't think we expected to see it within our lifetimes, but the Exalls showed they can advance at such an incredible pace. They passed us in terms of technology and their overall abilities. Hijacking peoples' minds? How the hell are we supposed to defend against that? I remember hearing about the Jonathon Browne incident a few years back—it was at that moment I had a long talk with my dad about the bunker, and to be ready to use it should the sky turn dark with jets. If one Exall could pull that off, it was only a matter of time until more could—then we'd have no chance."

"We could've kept fighting. We did well on the freeway."

Bernard chuckled, shaking his head. "Did well? Look at how many of us remain. There were *hundreds* of Crew members there that day. Now we have a dozen. That entire battle was a sham so the Exalls could infiltrate the building. They outplayed us, plain and simple. I know some of us may debate the need for Plan D so soon, but the Exalls called checkmate when they wiped out everyone at the Pentagon. They won the war after all these years. Plan D was only a natural progression from that bloody scene left behind."

"Yeah, that's a lot to think about, and I suppose it doesn't even matter at this point. It happened and here we are… nothing we can do about it now."

Bernard nodded, slowing the vehicle down as they officially entered St. Louis by crossing over the New Chain of Rocks Bridge, clear on the north side of town where the fallen debris hadn't collapsed the bridge.

"We're about five minutes away," Bernard said. "Should we wake them up now?"

Kyle looked over his shoulder to find Major Ortiz with his head cocked back, mouth agape as he snoozed the late hours away. Camille wasn't too different, her head leaning to the side instead. "Might as well wait til we get there."

Bernard shook his head. "I never thought I'd be coming back home under these circumstances. I haven't been here in seven years. My dad visited me lots of times in D.C. He was the one with all the free time and enjoyed traveling, so he'd come out and we'd see the sights and catch Nats games."

They left the bridge behind, turning off the freeway and into what used to be a neighborhood. The headlights splashed across the remnants, the area looking more like a tornado had struck it.

Enough remained to tell what they had built the houses from, both splinters of wood and crumbled bricks lying beneath piles of siding and roof shingles.

"Here we are," Bernard said, bringing the truck to a complete stop in front of a pile of bricks. He craned his neck as he stared out the windshield, confirming they were indeed at the correct property since the landscape looked the same in all directions.

He killed the engine, and the change of momentum caused Ortiz and Camille to wake up, yawning as they stretched their arms in unison.

"Rise and shine," Bernard said, opening his door and hopping out, immediately scanning the area for the bunker's flag. He clicked on a flashlight and started into the mess, everyone else finally hopping out to help. "I'm not finding anything."

"We're gonna have to dig," Camille said, her voice croaking after the extended nap.

"Unnecessary," Bernard called, already in the middle of the property, standing tall atop the remains of his father's home. "I can see the opening to the basement."

They all rushed over, Bernard grabbing a sheet of siding and tossing it aside, revealing a stairwell filled with dirt and rocks. The climb down didn't appear too difficult, but they'd still need to keep someone above ground just in case something toppled and covered the entry.

"I'm going in," Bernard said, not wasting a moment, holding cautiously onto the crumbling walls around him.

Kyle froze for a split second, torn between going down with Bernard or not. Fortunately, Camille bailed him out.

"I'll stay up here with Wells," she said. "We'll poke around the neighborhood and see if we can find anything."

Major Ortiz nodded without a word and promptly followed behind Bernard, both men disappearing into the darkness, their flashlights dancing around.

"Thanks," Kyle said to Camille, kicking some dirt aside. "How are you doing?"

"I'm okay, just shocked in a way that won't leave me. It would've been easier had my parents not been in the bunker at all. Then I could form my own conclusions about what happened and where they were. But that suicide note—"

Her lips trembled, and she squeezed her eyes shut, shaking her head vigorously from side to side.

"You don't have to hold anything back," Kyle said, debating if he should embrace his captain, and deciding not to.

Camille cleared her throat and looked back up to meet Kyle's gaze. "It's just hard not being able to explain it away. We know exactly what happened and I *hate* it. If they would've just waited, they'd be fine with us. Driving behind us like a caravan." A half moon provided just enough of a glow for Kyle to see the tears pooling over her irises. "This isn't the world I ever imagined living in."

Kyle considered what to say that might comfort Camille, but was interrupted by the heavy footsteps of Bernard and Ortiz making their way back up the stairwell. He exchanged a quick glance with Camille, concern on both of their faces that they only heard two sets of footsteps.

"Shit," Camille uttered under breath, surely understanding the pain Bernard was already feeling.

Their heads appeared like groundhogs popping out of the earth, their bodies promptly following behind.

Bernard gritted his teeth as he shook his head. "No one in there," he said, his voice emotionless. "I'm sure my dad wasn't even home—probably didn't have time to realize what was happening and make it back."

He paced around the remains of his father's home, moving in no intentional direction. In the silent night they could hear his breathing grow heavier with each step, increasing in rate as it flirted with hyperventilation.

"GOD DAMMIT!" he screamed, bending down to pick up what looked like a chunk of drywall, throwing it far into the distance. He kicked a small mound of bricks and kept lunging from spot to spot in a desperate search for something to destroy. After another minute of releasing his rage, Bernard collapsed knees-first onto the debris, thick streams of tears glistening under the moonlight. Ortiz rushed to his side, embracing him around the shoulders.

"I'm sorry, Bernard."

Bernard couldn't form any words, his face quivering as mucus and tears pooled at the tip of his nose and dripped to the ground in long, viscous strings.

"Let's get you out of here," Ortiz said, squatting over to lift Bernard from beneath the arms like a small child.

Struck by one last burst of rage, Bernard jumped to his feet and turned back to face the remnants of his father's home, puffing out his chest. "I'll kill every last one of you gray pieces of *shit*! I swear to God!"

As quickly as his energy had arrived, it also left. Bernard required every ounce of concentration and effort to walk away. His legs wobbly, they all helped him back into the truck without another word.

18

Chapter 18

As Robert Chapman finally mustered the courage to finish loading his car and hit the road for Denver, the squad of Crew members drove in a comfortable silence as they approached the Kansas border. They crossed the entire state of Missouri in four hours, having slowed down while they drove through Columbia, and spent thirty minutes in Kansas City where Major Ortiz had commented about the country concert that had sparked all this chaos.

Bernard emitted random bursts of crying, which prompted Camille to join him. The vehicle became an emotional train wreck on wheels, now half of them vulnerable to outbursts at any second. Kyle and Major Ortiz silently clung to their hopes of finding better news at their homes.

Reaching Denver, though, had become an urgent priority. Not even Ortiz had any concern for sifting through rubble in different towns. It had been two weeks since they left Washington—any survivors had already found safety of their own or died off.

They officially crossed the border into Kansas, the big blue welcome sign still intact. "Should be eight hours to Denver from here," Ortiz said, having resumed his favorite role behind the wheel. It was almost six in the morning, the sunrise chasing them from behind, and the announcement made Kyle's stomach flip.

Eight hours stood between him and a reunion with Sandra, and hopefully his father. They'd need to pull over to fill up the gas tank one time, of which they had passed enough diesel trucks to siphon from.

Having watched Camille and Bernard face their former hometowns and confronting the destruction, Kyle mentally prepared for his arrival to Larkwood. He closed his eyes and tried to imagine his grandmother's house crumbled to nothing, climbing into the debris in search of the flag connected to the bunker. He imagined finding it, tugging it to reach its core, and digging open the top hatch, swinging open the door where his father's eyes would look up, filled with joy at his arrival and rescue.

Please let him be in there. He had already accepted that his mother likely didn't make it, but until he received confirmation with his own eyes and drove by her home, he maintained hope. She didn't have a bunker, but should have had enough time to understand what was happening and flee to safety at Travis's house.

But he still played the odds over and over in his head, knowing Plan D was designed to leave behind one-one hundredth of a percent of the total population, or roughly 33,000 people. It was a meticulous and macabre plan to destroy all cities with a population over 30,000 residents, and leaving everyone else to die from the lack of basic resources. As sudden and drastic as the initial blow may have been, Plan D was really a three-month process designed to kill even the rural population in due time.

"How are you doing, Wells?" Ortiz asked over his shoulder, catching a glimpse of Kyle in the rearview mirror.

"I'd be lying if I said everything was fine. I'm really nervous about going home now."

"Understandable. A lot is riding on your grandmother's house, never mind the potential of us finding your father."

"Bernard," Kyle said. "I think we need to have a word before we arrive."

Bernard sat in the passenger seat, partly reclined from his brief nap earlier. He gazed at the truck's ceiling with bloodshot eyes, not moving. "Don't worry, kid, I'm not gonna kill your Exall until we're done with her."

"That's what I want to discuss—there's no reason to kill her at all. I know you have good reason to kill all Exalls—so do I—but this one is different. I can't emphasize that enough."

"Well, gee, Wells, should we bring her along in the truck with us? Maybe give her some of our precious food and water? Maybe give her an opportunity to drive us off a cliff?"

"I'm not saying any of that, and you know it," Kyle snapped. "All I'm asking is for an open mind."

"How about a vote?" Bernard asked, still moving nothing besides his lips.

"Don't drag me into this," Camille said.

"It's actually a fair proposal," Ortiz added. "It's best we prepare ahead for any potential decisions we have to make."

"It's my family's house," Kyle said. "Everything within it belongs to me. No one else has the right to tell me what to do with my belongings."

"Actually, if a live Exall is found, the Exall and all surrounding property are subject to possession of the Crew," Ortiz explained. "And since I'm currently the highest ranking official we have, I'm giving you the benefit of the doubt by allowing a vote instead of declaring total control over your grandmother's house. Technically, her basement bunker is property of the Crew as is, no permission is needed to extract anything from it, including any survivors."

Kyle's face flushed with anger. He bit his bottom lip before saying something that would surely get him kicked out of the Humvee.

"We have two options," Ortiz said. "We can either kill the Exall or bring her with us. There's no point in leaving a live Exall behind that might come back to hurt us down the road. She's part of our team, or an enemy—no in between. Now, this will depend on our encounter, as well, but let's have a sense of what we *want* to do."

"*I* want to put a slug in her head," Bernard said with a crooked grin. If Kyle didn't know any differently, he might have thought Bernard was drunk.

"I vote we keep her alive," Ortiz said, prompting Bernard to bolt upright from his reclined seat.

"What?! Major, I think you are rushing into your decision."

"And you're not? Monroe and Wells haven't even voted yet, so why are you so excited?"

"Well, I thought the most tenured person here would want to kill the Exall. Was that not our oath?" Bernard's brows furrowed in disbelief, eyes bulging beneath them.

"Our oath is to protect the country from all Exall attacks. Right now, we don't have much of a country, and we don't know if this Exall is a threat. That's regarding the oath. Our current mission is to restore civilization, and this Exall just might be useful in doing so. If she poses any threat, of course we will kill her, but until then, we need to see what she can offer."

"Are you listening to yourself?! This is an *Exall* we're talking about. She can control your mind, make you kill all of us if she really wanted. There is absolutely no reason to put us all at risk so that some rookie doesn't get his feelings hurt."

"That's bullshit and you know it," Ortiz said through gritted teeth. "Captain Monroe, please share your vote."

Camille shifted in the seat next to Kyle, shooting him a look that was either dirty or concerned—he couldn't tell. She looked forward before speaking. "I vote we keep the Exall alive."

Bernard let out a long sigh, shaking his head, slumping back into his seat like a punished child.

"We've always wanted a live Exall to study," she continued. "Regardless of what's going on in the world right now, it would be irresponsible to pass up this opportunity. I think we should plan to spend an extended amount of time in Denver to really get to the bottom of what this Exall can offer. What if we have the chance to solve the very existence of the Exall species? That would mean we could learn how to eliminate them. We all understand there are risks, but Kyle said she is strapped to a table, and has been for a long time. If Susan Wells made it as far as she did, then I have no concern about us going in there ready to learn. My only concern, Major, is the delay this may cause to keep you from getting home."

"I'll be fine. I've already thought things over. This is our top priority now. And what is your formal vote, Wells?" Ortiz asked, eyes focused on him in the mirror.

"To keep her alive, of course."

"That settles it then, three votes to one."

"Ah, that's right, democracy never got anyone killed," Bernard said. "How silly of me to forget. You can all go in there and play games with this Exall. I'll wait outside. If you want to bring me files to review, then fine, but don't expect me to approach the alien."

"We will discuss logistics when we get there," Ortiz said. "We still have eight hours ahead of us. Now let's take a moment to cool off and get in the proper mindset for what lies ahead."

19

Chapter 19

Robert didn't have the restrictions of needing to stop in particular cities to check for life, so he made much greater time than the caravan ahead of him. He had calculated needing to fill up his gas tank at least three times between Dayton and Denver, bringing a hose with him to siphon from any other cars he passed by. He had seen a handful once he got outside the city and it appeared the rural areas had been less affected by the demolition. Yes, he wanted to stop at some of the nearby barns as he drove past, convinced there were others, but he needed to reach his son and know he was okay. Anything that impeded would likely meet the end of his shotgun, which coincidentally rode shotgun in the Ford Focus.

"Aliens, government goons, survivors," he repeated to keep himself engaged while driving on the open road. He had just stopped for gas in the middle of nowhere in Illinois. It was a painful transfer of gasoline for Robert, taking it from a beautiful Dodge Ram pickup truck. He wasted at least three minutes standing between the truck and the Focus, debating if it was worth it to transfer all the food and belongings. He decided against, knowing it would both waste time and cause more stops along the way as the truck was less fuel-efficient. Robert needed to get to Denver as quickly as possible. Perhaps he would find a new vehicle once he arrived there.

If he encountered either aliens or government workers, he planned to shoot them and proceed. Neither deserved his time or attention. Should he encounter a fellow survivor, he'd take a moment to gauge their personality and weigh if they might be of any assistance on the remainder of the trip. If they didn't, or needed help themselves, he'd throw them a can of food and be on his way. Robert now found himself as a kind soul in a depressing world. He needed to adapt if he wanted any chance of survival.

The Humvee that had nearly caught him in Dayton had to surely be in Colorado by now, if not further. As easy as it was to zone out while being the only vehicle on the wide open freeway, Robert snapped himself into focus every couple of minutes to ensure he had his eyes looking far ahead for any movement. He didn't know where they were stopping or for how long. All he knew was the general direction they had left Dayton, and had to assume they were headed west. He also kept his eyes on the rearview mirror, worried the alien he had encountered at the Foster property was on his tail.

"No way they know how to drive a car," he said to reassure himself, but not really believing it. If an alien species found a way to Earth and created so much chaos, driving a vehicle was likely a simple task for them to learn.

"They can do everything," a gentle voice cooed from the passenger seat, startling Robert to the point of swerving the car, cans of food clattering and rolling around the trunk.

"What the hell?!" he gasped, looking to his right and seeing his late wife sitting there, the shotgun held in her grasp. "Jenny?"

Speaking his wife's name out loud made chills break down his back, perhaps more so than actually seeing her. *I'm hallucinating, that's all. Been a long few weeks in isolation, and this is how the mind plays tricks.*

He squeezed his eyes shut for a brief second and shook his head, opening them to find Jenny still sitting in the passenger seat, as if she had been there the whole time.

"Don't worry, Rob," she said with a kind smirk. "You're not going crazy. I am part of your subconscious. I'm really just a part of you."

Tears ran down Robert's cheeks as he fought to split his attention between the road ahead and the reincarnation of his wife next to him. His heart hammered, adrenaline flooding his senses to the point of dizziness. He slammed on the brakes and swerved to the side of the road, his trunk certainly as much of a mess as the big cities he had driven by.

Jenny held the grab handle above, the shotgun remaining safely in her possession.

"I'm so sorry," Robert said, trying to gather his thoughts. "I had to pull over. I can't process what is happening right now—I feel like I might faint."

"Oh, Rob, I'm just here to keep you company and to wish you luck finding Gavin—he needs it, and if you don't make it there sooner, he'll be gone."

"What do you mean? He was headed for safety when I called him."

"You were right about this whole thing, but some things you got wrong. The airport in Denver isn't what you think. Gavin needs you—he only has a few hours left."

Hundreds of thoughts rushed through Robert's mind as he sat on the side of the freeway. He wanted to ask what all she knew about Gavin, but also had so many questions for Jenny regarding her last days alive. And if she really was part of his mind, what did that mean going forward? Would he be able to summon her as he pleased, or was this a momentary event that his exhausted and paranoid brain was filling on its own?

Her words created their own sense of urgency, further strengthening Robert's need to reach Denver and not waste time doing anything else. He decided, against every desire in his body, to set aside his questions regarding Jenny's death.

"How long do I have you?" he asked, reaching out and watching in dismay as his hand moved through her body like a hologram.

"Not much longer. Seeing me has sparked a reaction in your brain. I'll be gone very soon."

"Where is Gavin?"

"He's at the Denver airport, trapped under rubble. He's been roaming around, got lucky and found a few water bottles, but hasn't had any food since all of this. Right now he's lying down, unable to move. He's been that way for the last three days, skin sinking into his bones. He'll be gone by the morning, for sure, possibly sooner."

"Will I see you again?" Robert asked, sensing his time with his wife already coming to a close. She kept staring forward, distracted, not reciprocating the affection Robert wanted in this moment. Maybe she had her own rules to play by. Maybe he was in fact completely crazy.

"Don't count on it," she said, still avoiding eye contact. "Once you reach Denver, everything will change. You'll be too occupied to even think of me."

"Jenny, I will never stop thinking of you."

She turned her head with the gentlest smile and nodded. "You really need to go. The next time you blink, I'll be gone."

Robert accepted the challenge and kept his eyes open for about forty-five seconds until they itched. When his eyelids closed and reopened, Jenny was indeed gone without a trace. He broke into a heavy cry, heaving as tears fell to his legs and soaked through his pants. His chest became hollow, much like it had the day of Jenny's funeral. It was an emptiness he had learned to live with and push aside, but seeing her brought it all back, and returned him to square one with his grieving. Now he'd torment himself for the rest of the trip, wondering why she didn't express her love for him, regretting that he didn't attempt to truly touch her, embrace her, smell her hair and taste her lips. The opportunity slipped through his fingers like sand.

He took an extra five minutes to regain his composure, putting the car back into gear and pulling off the side of the road. Denver may as well have been on another planet, but he needed to get there just the same. Gavin needed him, and no one had needed him in quite a while.

"I love you," Robert said, looking at the now empty seat next to him, the shotgun appearing untouched. He accepted that his brief encounter wasn't truly real, but insisted it was more than mere imagination. There had been plenty of accounts where spirits visited their loved ones, and even some where they came back to warn others of what lie ahead. "If you were in my imagination, then I'd have you visit every day."

He shook his head while gaining speed, knowing that the subconscious was completely out of his control. The rest of the trip would have plenty of prayer as Robert fought to make sense, and peace, of what had just happened.

By the time he reached the Illinois border and passed St. Louis, a wide smile stuck to his face, memories of his late wife flooding his mind. The open road lay ahead, and with it plenty of uncertainty. But he had just left the most important soul behind him and looked forward to reuniting with his son.

"Only twelve more hours."

20

Chapter 20

The stretch through Kansas and eastern Colorado had been boring as usual, but as they inched closer toward downtown, it grew apparent the city of Denver was gone. Kyle's eyes welled with tears at the sight. Seeing all the prior cities had been overwhelming, but none were places he was familiar with. Gone was the iconic Cash Register Building, as the locals knew it, and its surrounding skyscrapers. All that remained was the majestic Rocky Mountains in the distance, glowing bright blue in the sunny afternoon.

"Which way are we going?" Ortiz asked, the Humvee cruising along I-70.

Kyle opened his mouth to speak, having to first fight a lump in his throat. They were fifteen minutes away from his father's house, and that made his guts boil in angst. It had been a mental preparation long in the making, but the time had finally come for him to face the truth of whether Travis had survived the attacks. Much like Bernard had, he braced for the worst, while hoping something would finally go right for this squad.

Ortiz pulled off the interstate, exiting into Larkwood, where nothing from Kyle's childhood remained. His entire body tensed as he looked left to right, his brain filling in what should have been there.

Kyle rolled down his window, wanting both a better view, but also a sense of the smells and sounds of his hometown. All the other cities they had passed through had a distinct stench of burnt wood. Larkwood was no different, although the odor had faded away in the weeks since the bombings.

"Sorry, Wells," Bernard said from the front. He knew exactly the feelings rushing through Kyle's mind, and didn't need to say anything more.

Kyle's head spun, the tension not lifting as they inched closer to his father's home. They turned onto the block, his mother's house clearly demolished as they passed her street.

Okay, Mom is gone, he thought, eyes welling.

They slowed down after a few seconds, and Kyle hung his head out the window as they pulled up to the property that was once his grandmother's. The house lay in shambles, some of the roof shingles spilling into the street.

"Here we are," Ortiz announced, killing the engine. He paused a moment, checking over his shoulder before opening the door and hopping out. Camille promptly followed, leaving Kyle and Bernard alone in the vehicle.

"I know things got heated earlier," Bernard said. "I still don't agree with any of this, but I just want to wish you good luck in there. I'll be standing guard outside, but please know I've been thinking positive thoughts for you. I can't imagine going through all of this at your age. I gotta admit—I admire you, Wells."

"Thanks. You've been the closest thing to a friend since I've joined the Crew."

"We're family," Bernard replied with a wink. "And don't you forget it. Let's get out of here and see what we're dealing with."

Bernard swung his door open, and Kyle followed suit with plenty of reluctance. Ortiz and Camille waited at the top of what used to be the driveway, the major with his hands on his waist as he looked down to the pile of rubble. "Do you know what area the bunker would be in?"

Kyle knew precisely where it was, made his way toward it, taking careful steps over splintered wood and broken glass. His grandmother's presence radiated from the rubble, tickling the gooseflesh down his back. He wondered if she had somehow known this was the future that awaited, prompting her to act almost carelessly in her last stand against the Exalls.

Kyle reached the area of the bunker and started throwing debris to the side. Everyone else joined him, clearing the path in the area until Kyle dropped his boot down with a hollow thud. "I got it!"

He revealed the old freezer chest that he had crawled down four years earlier. The freezer itself wasn't the prize they were looking for, but the hatch that it concealed underneath it. The freezer was too heavy for Kyle to move on his own, so Bernard climbed over to help hoist it aside, sending it clattering down a small hill where it crashed to its final resting place next to the street.

The hatch showed its dark gray wheel, and Kyle dropped to a knee and turned it. Once it popped open, his father's voice called out from below, "Kyle, is that you?!"

Kyle threw the hatch wide open and locked eyes with Travis. "Oh my God!" Kyle cried, slapping his hand over his mouth. "Dad? Is it really you? Am I seeing things?"

Travis looked up, his smile from ear to ear. "It's me, Ky. I made it."

Those words were the pin that popped the balloon of tension for Kyle, relief immediately shattering his every paranoid, negative thought. The rest of his squad hurried around him, mouths agape as they looked down and saw the first human looking back at them since the world had gone dark.

"Mr. Wells," Ortiz said, squatting down. "Do you require any medical assistance? Food or water?"

"No, sir," Travis called back. "I'm all set in here."

Ortiz stood up, grinning as he looked at Kyle. "This is great news, kid."

Kyle looked around, still speechless. Camille watched with her hands on her cheeks, tears rolling down her face. Kyle supposed she was playing her traumatic experience over in her head, longing for this same chance to greet her parents.

"Is anyone else in there?" Kyle asked, knowing it was unlikely.

Travis dropped his head toward the ground. "I called your mother when this all happened. She was meeting with a vendor in Boulder. Wanted me to tell you she loves you, and is incredibly proud of the man you've become."

Kyle's face flushed upon hearing these words, his bottom lip quivering. As much as he had mentally and emotionally prepared to face his mother's death, the reality hit just as hard as it would under normal circumstances. She knew her death was unavoidable, reserving her last words for Kyle. He was glad that Travis survived to pass along the message—it provided some closure that he'd need on the late nights of crying that lie ahead.

Ortiz put an arm around Kyle's shoulder. "Shall we head

down?"

Kyle nodded, wiping away the tears with his sleeve. In that moment, he had forgotten all about Sandra and the hours of research that awaited them. His mother was gone, and he felt the urge to do *something*, but had no idea what.

"You still want to stand guard out here?" Ortiz asked Bernard, who replied with a nod. "Okay, let's have the rest of us go down. We'll try to get you some files to analyze."

"Sounds good, boss," Bernard said, taking a step back from the open hatch to allow Camille easier access.

They each crawled down the ladder, descending into the bunker as the tension in the air grew thicker by the second. They understood they were about to face a tipping point in their survival plans, and experience something no Crew member had before. Except for Susan Wells and Kyle.

When he reached the ground first, Kyle threw his arms around Travis, squeezing his father while a fresh wave of tears made their rounds for both of them.

"I'm so sorry about your mom," Travis whispered while Ortiz and Camille climbed down. He pulled back to meet Kyle's gaze, only able to shake his head.

"I can't believe this is happening," Kyle cried, losing all control again. All the emotions he had kept bottled up since the bombs dropped were fully unleashed now that he had the comfort of his remaining family.

They held each other for another minute before Kyle pulled back, wiping his eyes clear again.

"Mr. Wells," Ortiz said. "I'm glad to see you make it this far. How have things been?"

Travis nodded. "Considering the world is gone, I'd say things have been okay. The bunker worked exactly how my mom always said it would. I'm grateful I listened to her all those years and learned her routines for keeping it stocked and ready."

"Have you had any encounters with the Exall?"

Travis scrunched his face, prompting Kyle to step forward. "He doesn't know about it."

"Know about what?" Travis asked, looking at all three faces in front of him. Camille had been strolling around the bunker, checking out its setup, but stopped to join Ortiz once he started asking questions. "Ky?"

Kyle didn't respond, instead shuffling away from the group and toward the wall behind them. "Behind here is a hidden laboratory," he said, nodding to the wall. "I found it by total accident one day when I was down here. Grandma left some files in those cabinets—I read through them and found a message she left for me."

Travis looked to the only file cabinet in the room, shaking his head. "I've been down here for how long now? I opened that cabinet once, flipped through a couple files and got bored very quick." He chuckled. "So there's an alien living behind this wall?"

Kyle nodded. "Her name is Sandra, and she's been with Grandma for a long time. She was being studied, and they became friends, I guess. I'm still not clear how that relationship worked, but Sandra was expecting me. Grandma told her I would find her one day."

"Unreal," Travis said, unable to look away from the wall.

"Mr. Wells, as you can imagine, this is highly sensitive information—"

"Oh, don't worry, I know to not tell a soul, or else." He grinned and made a gun with his fingers, pulling the trigger next to his head. "Wait, weren't there four of you?" He looked back up through the open hatch.

"Franzen is waiting outside," Ortiz explained. "We always leave someone outside just in case something were to fall and block our way out. And he isn't exactly thrilled about us having a talk with the Exall. You're welcome to climb up and wait with him—I'm sure he'd love the company."

"I'd like to take a look inside this lab. Just curious to see what kind of secret life my mother was living, if that's okay."

"Fine with me," Ortiz said. "But I must urge you to tell us if you start feeling different. We don't know what we're dealing with exactly, and just need to be cautious."

"Understood."

"Are we ready then?" Ortiz asked, Kyle nodding his head.

"Let's do it," Camille said, speaking for the first time in the bunker. She shouted up the hatch to let Bernard know they were heading in, and he popped his head into sight, giving a thumbs up and wishing them luck.

They gathered around Kyle, who took a step closer to the wall, making his eyes bulge so the hidden scanner could read them. After a few seconds, the wall started vibrating and slid open, revealing a dark hallway.

21

Chapter 21

The hallway was just as Kyle remembered; he led the way with Ortiz, Camille, and Travis following behind in a single-file line.

"Kyle? Is that you?" Sandra's gentle voice called out.

Ortiz whipped out his pistol, cocking it without hesitation. Kyle waved a hand for him to put it down, but the major didn't care.

Kyle didn't know why his legs trembled as he continued forward, turning the sharp corner where the soft glow of lights from the lab came into sight. He worried that Ortiz or Camille might harm Sandra without giving a proper chance to see what she could offer.

He stopped a step shy of entering the lab, Sandra visible and still strapped to the table, just as he had left her several weeks earlier. "Don't approach her too quickly—let me go in and explain who you all are."

Ortiz nodded, Camille craning her neck around his enormous frame for a look at the Exall. Her mouth opened, but she said nothing.

Kyle entered the lab as Sandra rolled her head to the side and locked eyes with him. "I told you I'd be back," he said.

Her black eyes gazed, dark hair outspread behind her head. "Thank you, Kyle. Your grandmother was right about you—a good person. Who are these people you brought?"

"They're with me—they just want to help. Major Ortiz and Captain Monroe work with me in the Crew, just like my grandmother. And the other man is my father, Travis."

"Travis?" she asked, lifting her head for a clearer look. Travis took a step behind Camille, hiding like a shy child. "I've heard so much about you, Travis," Sandra said, laying her head back down, talking as if no one in the room held any fear. "Your mother told me so many stories from your childhood. You look like her—has anyone told you that?"

Travis couldn't help but grin at the compliment, and stepped back into the open. "As a matter of fact, yes. Thank you." His words came out slow and awkward, unsure if he could respond.

"Would you like to meet everyone?" Kyle asked her.

"That would be lovely."

Kyle turned and waved them over, Ortiz taking the first step, eyes glued on Sandra. They all stood next to Kyle, stretching from Sandra's head to feet. Kyle watched the other three as they stood in amazed silence. It reminded Kyle of the first time he entered the Sistine Chapel, overwhelming and impossible to look away.

He knew Major Ortiz was experiencing the same sensation with a living Exall in front of him, looking back at him, thinking, speaking, emoting.

"Hello," Sandra said to the major, her eyes burning into his gaze.

Camille stood near the Exall's feet, staring in amazement.

"This is incredible," Ortiz said, shaking his head. "I never thought in a million years I'd have an opportunity like this. Where are you from?"

"This is the only home I remember," Sandra said. "I came here as a child, and Susan saved me. I've lived most of my life in this room."

"Do you know any capabilities you have? Can you communicate with others outside of this room?"

"I used to communicate with Susan. Her and I could chat while she was upstairs. I think she did a test once and talked to me as far as a mile away. I'm not sure of what else I can do. Susan did so many tests with me, I can't recall, plus it was so long ago."

"Just fascinating," Ortiz said again, taking a step back and scanning the room of all its file cabinets. "Sandra, this is a big hypothetical, but if we were to take you out of here and back into the world, would you be able to sense if there are other Exalls around?"

"I can. I just don't know how far of a range. The day of the attacks at Kyle's school, I sensed them nearby. Susan was also communicating with me, so I'm not sure if that factors in."

"How close was your school?" Ortiz asked, whipping his head over to Kyle.

"It's—it *was* just a block over."

"Damn. Anything helps, but I wish we knew more."

"It's all in these files, Major. Take my word—I only got to flip through a few, but they're all loaded with information."

"Major," Camille said, speaking for the first time in front of the Exall. "If Susan could communicate with Sandra from a distance, that could only mean one thing."

Ortiz nodded. "Yep, she had Exall blood in her system—no other explanation."

Kyle furrowed his brow in deep thought. The textbook knowledge he had learned was still rather fresh in his mind. He couldn't recall this direct conclusion, but remembered that Exalls tried to get their blood into humans as a way of controlling them. Would his grandmother really have done it to herself? Or did Sandra attack her before getting strapped to the table, Susan keeping it a secret all these years? The possibility left more questions than answers, sparking new theories for them to digest.

The idea worried him about what other revelations awaited inside the file cabinets. It was entirely possible that Susan had learned valuable information about the Exall species that had never been shared with the Crew, something Major Ortiz was sure to have a heyday with.

"You have secrets inside you," Ortiz said to Sandra, staring into her gray soul. "We have to find out what they are—they can change the world."

Sandra grinned, a chilling revelation of the black teeth that lied beneath her crooked smile. She said nothing, leaving the room in an awkward silence until Camille spoke.

"We should get started, Major. We're going to be here awhile."

Ortiz nodded, forcing his eyes to look another direction, falling on Kyle who had taken a step back from the table. "This is as good as advertised, Wells. I'll admit, I had some doubts about what we'd find. I didn't think you were making it up—I guess I just didn't think it was real until I saw with my own eyes."

"I understand, Major. Imagine my dilemma when I had just found her down here and Colonel Griffins called me back to D.C. I wanted to tell him, but had no idea if he'd even believe me.

We had plans to come out here after the battle."

Ortiz crossed his arms and returned his attention to Sandra. "Did you know about the battle? Was it part of some plan by your kind?"

"I know nothing about what is taking place above ground. I sensed lots of doom and fear and felt the tremors of the Earth. I know of no plans for such madness. Our goal was always to peacefully exist alongside humans."

"Then why do Exalls murder humans so often? Seems kind of hard for humans to take you seriously about living peacefully."

"We are no different than yourselves. We have good and bad within our species. Sometimes the bad cry out much louder for attention. My father was good, but he had some brothers who were not. You must understand how our species has traveled through the universe in search of a planet to live. We never wanted to encroach on your lives, just wanted to find a way to blend in."

"Then why do you come back every thirty years?" Camille asked. "Why does it seem like a constant cycle of battles against you? Why has an Exall never approached a human and asked how to go about living here?"

Sandra sighed disappointment. "Our technology allows us to watch your planet from afar. We study the human species, see how you react to certain scenarios. We understand an alien species arriving on Earth would cause mayhem. It would also endanger us. We have bad ones in our leadership positions. They like to come down every now and then to see if the planet is any closer to being rid of humans, so they try to wipe out as many as they can during their visits."

"So there really are peaceful Exalls around the world," Ortiz whispered to himself. The Crew had long known of roughly fifty Exalls who lived in isolation around the globe, minding their business and never disturbing a human life. "We have a lot to learn from you."

"I'm happy to help as much as I can, but keep in mind my knowledge has limits, as I've lived down here as long as I can remember."

"We need to focus on the files," Kyle reminded Ortiz once more. "Sandra can only tell us so much—I know my grandma stored mountains of valuable info in this room."

"Let's get to it," Ortiz said. "Let's each take a wall and start. Open the cabinets and really take the time to read through all the notes. A lot of it may be technical, or things we may already know, so let's make separate piles of existing knowledge and new knowledge. If there's anything that seems urgent, please share with the group immediately."

"Do you want me involved in this?" Travis asked.

"Certainly. If you wouldn't mind running some files up to Bernard outside, he wanted to help with this portion and can do so from his current post."

"On it."

Travis moved first, wasting no time in claiming the wall closest to the exit to give him a shorter trip back and forth. He promptly opened a drawer, grabbed an armful of files, and disappeared from the laboratory.

Major Ortiz crossed the room to the opposite side of Sandra, gazing at the wall of cabinets as if perusing a store, eventually deciding to start at the far left.

Camille and Kyle went their separate ways, and the room fell into a rather calming silence while they all sifted through documents, the only audible sound that of papers ruffling and flipping.

"Wow," Ortiz said. "Sandra has been down here since the 90's, almost three full decades. How did Susan keep this a secret for so long?"

"How did Sandra never show up on a tracking device?" Camille asked. "Because if anyone spotted an Exall at the same location as a Crew member, they would have sent in a team for a rescue mission immediately."

"Susan had been injecting me with human blood for our entire time together," Sandra said. "She believed there was a way to transform me into a human through some sort of genetic manipulation. She didn't share too many of her results with me, but mentioned my body temperature had risen to nearly human levels."

"That explains it," Ortiz said. The tracking devices used a thermal energy sensor to detect organisms with a much lower internal temperature, much like the Exalls. If Susan had raised that temperature, Sandra would never have been sensed by the devices. "Sandra, do you know if there is any sort of structure or order to these file cabinets?"

"Unfortunately, no. Susan never told me much about them—I only saw her open and close them often."

Ortiz nodded and returned his attention to the file in hand. The three of them kept digging for answers, Travis making his rounds back and forth to deliver an entire cabinet to Bernard, handfuls of files at a time.

"It's gonna be a long couple of days," Kyle said, flipping through a document of theories why the Exalls sought to bring so much mayhem to Earth.

Chapter 22

They spent four hours sifting through files before breaking to eat, joining Bernard outside for a luxurious meal of ham and turkey sandwiches. Compared to eating out of cans during the entirety of their road trip, they suddenly felt like royalty. Major Ortiz also talked Bernard down from his rage, and convinced him to join them in the bunker, at least. He didn't need to step foot inside the laboratory if he didn't want to.

Bernard had spent most of his time clearing the area of rubble, since they would all sleep in the bunker.

The vibe inside the bunker reminded Kyle of slumber parties he used to have with friends as a younger teenager. They took advantage of not having to sleep in a car or tent for the first time in weeks, everyone changing into the lone pair of pajamas they had packed. Despite spending the entire day and evening underground, a sense of normalcy had returned. Susan's bunker had been connected to several power generators, equipped to last at least six months, according to notes found in their initial research.

After a half day of sorting through the file cabinets, Major

Ortiz predicted at least a week for them to look through all the notes Susan had accumulated. The bunker was more comfortable than the laboratory, folding chairs and a blowout mattress available. Travis offered to give up the mattress, but everyone declined, insisting this was his home and he had first rights to anything he wished.

They also felt more relaxed working away from Sandra, so they each rolled a file cabinet into the bunker where they sat around and read together, speaking aloud when something interesting arose. Travis had a battery-operated CD player and a book of discs ranging across all genres. He put on soft rock to help their collective focus.

Dinner had long been done as the sun set over Larkwood. Kyle sat next to his dad in a folding chair. Ortiz, Camille, and Bernard spread out in different corners of the room that they had claimed as their spots for sleeping later.

Kyle longed for a moment alone with his father, but wasn't sure the best way to break away from the group. They couldn't exactly venture to the lab, where Sandra would surely listen. Even the hallway that led to the lab was too dark, leaving them unable to see each other. It might have to wait until tomorrow, where they could both slip outside for a few minutes.

"Holy shit!" Ortiz barked, jumping up from his chair, waving a sheet of paper in the air. "I've been suspecting it, but didn't think I'd actually read something to confirm it."

"What's the matter?" Camille asked, rising to her feet.

"Susan Wells injected herself with Exall blood from Sandra," he said, eyes glued to the paper. "After she captured Sandra and brought her to this lab, she extracted blood and ran tests for two years, trying to learn what was inside the blood, if there are ways to dilute it, or even ways to replace it with human blood. She studied how the bloods reacted together under a microscope, and concluded that mixing Exall blood to human blood at a 15 to 1 ratio would enable the human blood to remain the prominent DNA, but also allowed a portal into the DNA of Exalls. She had no choice but to try this experiment on herself.

"She shackled herself for two weeks in the lab, just in case anything took a wayward turn, but it never did. From here, she developed the ability of telepathically communicating with Sandra, even tested their link by inflicting pain on herself and seeing if Sandra could feel it—and she did. Sandra definitely felt something when Susan was killed."

"Wait, so if my grandma is alive still, Sandra might know?" Kyle asked, exchanging a concerned look with Travis.

"Ky, she's not alive—we all saw what happened," Travis said, patting an arm on his son's back. "She was shot and wasn't moving."

"I know, but they took her body. What if they have her strapped to a table somewhere, just like we have Sandra? What if they have ways of resurrecting a dead body?"

Kyle knew the thought was absurd, a desperate reach perhaps, but was it really such a drastic leap considering an alien species had pushed humanity to the brink of exterminating itself? Or was it crazier than having a live Exall hidden in a basement laboratory for nearly three decades?

"Wells," Major Ortiz said. "I know you want it to be true—and I won't rule it out as possible—but even if it is, we have no way of tracking down *where* she could be, let alone how to reach her."

"We have Sandra—they share a bond. How is no one else seeing this possibility?"

"It's right here in the notes," Ortiz said, raising the stack of papers he had been studying. "She tested the range of their communication, just like Sandra told us. They found they could communicate within a mile radius. Unless Susan's body is in this neighborhood, Sandra has no way of communicating with her. Plus, she said she sensed when Susan was in trouble and died. Don't you think if there was a possibility of her being alive that Sandra would have mentioned it? She loves your grandmother. That's clear."

"I don't know what to believe. I'm having a hard time wrapping my head around all of this." Kyle shrugged and sank back into his chair. "Let's just keep going through these files and maybe we'll find something that suggests this is possible."

Camille and Bernard had kept to themselves during Kyle's brief hysterics, exchanging glances and pretending to keep their attention focused on the papers in front of them. Travis kept a hand on Kyle's back, hoping his mere presence would help settle his son's nerves.

Major Ortiz declined to speak further, instead slipping his reading glasses back on and continuing his deep dive into Susan's notes. Kyle held a paper in his hand. Something about the psychological history of mind reading and mind control. His grandmother was certainly well-versed in topics all across the spectrum, but he had a hard time keeping his eyes open while scanning over her notes.

They returned to silence; the music drifting softly from the speakers. Kyle needed a moment to gather his thoughts and stepped away to the dark hallway. His emotions had been all over the place since arriving to find Travis alive. The problem for him, ever since leaving D.C., was how fake life felt. As if moving through a dream he couldn't wake up from, that constant cloudy feeling following him everywhere he went.

His mother was dead, leaving his chest a hollow pit. The reality dodged him, his mind and emotions too consumed. He knew the sorrow would creep up and wrap its fingers around his throat and only hoped it wouldn't happen at an inopportune moment.

"Captain Monroe," Ortiz said, startling Kyle from the silence. "I need to have a word with you in private." The major stood and clasped the file shut, turning into the dark hallway that had apparently become a safe space for anyone who needed a moment of seclusion.

Camille looked up and frowned, shooting a glance around the room before following Ortiz.

"That's not good," Bernard said once he was sure they were out of range to hear him.

"What do you mean?" Kyle asked.

"I've been around these two a long time now. Whenever they go off to an abrupt meeting, there's something important to discuss. The major really likes to groom Camille, has always seen her as a natural fit for a job like his. It usually involves a decision—but it's impossible to even guess what that would be under these circumstances."

Kyle leaned forward, suddenly nauseous. He didn't know why, but some deep layer in his conscious told him it was regarding him. It was his grandmother's files, after all.

His eyes darted to the dark opening of the tunnel, waiting for the two to emerge and reveal their secrets. But perhaps they wouldn't say anything. Not everything had to be a major decision that required action. Kyle reminded himself of this to settle down, but his mind kept spinning with possibilities. He returned to the file in his lap, reading it but not comprehending a single word.

Shortly after, the echo of footsteps carried out of the hallway, followed by Major Ortiz and Camille. Ortiz eyed Kyle before looking around the room. Kyle kept his head down, despite trying to steal a quick glance.

"Kyle, can you come here for a second, please?" Ortiz asked.

Kyle looked up with his brow furrowed, always noting the rarest of instances when Ortiz addressed him by his first name. He could think back and count on one hand how many times that had happened.

Stay calm, he thought. *This doesn't mean anything bad, could just be a question.*

He noticed his father's look of concern as he strolled across the room to meet Ortiz. "What's going on, Major?" Kyle asked, looking up to the behemoth of a man.

Ortiz shot a look over to Camille, and she reached out to snatch Kyle's left arm in unison with Ortiz grabbing his right.

"Hey, what the fuck?!" Kyle shouted, trying to wriggle out of their grip. They both pulled each arm behind him, the cold metal of handcuffs smacking around his wrists, before they lowered him to the ground where Ortiz kept hold as Kyle kicked and screamed.

"Calm down, Wells," Ortiz said, his tone undisturbed. "Relax, and I can tell you what's going on."

Travis and Bernard both shot out of their chairs, Travis leaping for Kyle, Bernard diving between him and his son.

"What the hell are you people doing?!" Travis cried as he hit the ground.

"Look, I don't know what's going on," Bernard said, "but it's best to hear the Major out."

"Bullshit! Let go of my son!" Travis kicked and twisted, but was no match for Bernard. He kept in decent shape but had nowhere near the amount of strength and power as any of the trained Crew members in the room, Kyle included.

"Everyone sit down!" Ortiz barked. "There's no need for us to fight—just let me explain what I read."

The major didn't use it often, but he held his drill sergeant tone for special occasions, sure to command respect from all corners of the room.

Kyle felt the pressure of Ortiz's beefy arms pressing into his side.

Travis didn't return to his chair, instead leaning against the wall with Bernard by his side. Both men panted for air as if they had just run a mile.

"Thank you," Ortiz continued. "Kyle, you're not in any sort of trouble, so please relax and listen. Your grandmother mentioned in her notes how she injected herself with Exall blood. It appears she did the same to you."

"What?!" Travis gasped. "What about me?!"

"There is no mention of you, Mr. Wells, but I am curious to draw some blood to be sure. It's possible she mentioned you in a different file, but Susan made it pretty clear that Kyle was the chosen one to continue her work long after her death."

"Chosen?" Kyle asked, still offering a weak fight behind his back to get out of the cuffs. "Chosen for what?"

"She ran those tests on herself and liked the results. She believed that if we could truly master this technique of extracting the precise amount of Exall blood and injecting it into humans, then we'd have the upper hand against them forever. This would allow us a better grasp on how to develop similar abilities to Exalls without triggering anything on the tracking devices."

"She called it The Mirror Method—Mirroring, for short," Camille said. "She never shared a single detail about her experiments with anyone in the Crew. Colonel Griffins would have probably hijacked the whole thing, both out of concern and curiosity. No one in our government was ready for that sort of experiment, especially considering we'd never had a live Exall in our possession. Your grandma took a huge gamble—she was lucky nothing ever went sour."

"So then it worked," Bernard said. "We've all heard the legend of Susan Wells and how she could sniff out an Exall attack before our own intelligence registered a threat. She listened to the Exalls around her and beat them to the punch."

"Correct," Ortiz said. "And that's what makes this ground-breaking. She actually cracked the code of defeating the Exalls. But the bigger question lingers. How did she end up getting killed by them? Her death was so simple—it makes no sense for her to have been caught off guard in her own house."

"She was saving us—saving Kyle," Travis said. "I remember like it was yesterday. She made us go into her bunker right after the attacks at Kyle's school. She knew the danger without even being there. She actually left the school early, before the attacks. Remember that, Kyle?"

That day of the basketball banquet seemed a million years in the past, but Kyle vividly remembered talking with his grandmother after the ceremony. She had left before they served the food, citing a need to get to work.

"I remember," Kyle said. "Brian killed her. She fought off the other two Exalls, but it was like she didn't know Brian was there."

"He was still very much human," Ortiz said. "Too recently infected for a complete transformation."

Kyle nodded again. "That makes sense. Which, if that's the case, did the Exalls know about her ability, and try to counter it with an Exall with more human blood in their system? It was all a giant chess match, and she didn't know all the rules yet."

"And that's why I handcuffed you," Ortiz said. "Like I mentioned, you're not in trouble—I just want to know what we're dealing with. What if Sandra's long game was to hijack your body? Use you as a weapon to break her free? We can't take any chances. Every move has to be thoroughly calculated."

"I agree," Kyle said, with less reluctance. "Let's back to reading these files and figure it all out."

23

Chapter 23

Two days had passed since Robert had spotted the government people disappear into a bunker in Larkwood, Colorado. He had gotten lucky by not getting too close, seeing them as a blip on the freeway ahead while driving outside of the Colorado border. He had wondered how he caught up to them so quickly, but figured they made stops on the way.

He found it plenty difficult tailing someone in the middle of open, flat land. The only thing that worried him was if they were hiding from something. What all did these people know? And why did they suddenly stop in this town to hide underground for a couple of days?

Robert planned to come back and check on them, but today was dedicated to finding his son at Denver International Airport only a thirty-minute drive east of Larkwood. The binoculars he had packed came in handy, allowing him to hide far in the distance, having taken shelter behind a mound of rubble. He stressed over the prospect of finding Gavin harmed, Jenny's words pushing Robert all the way to Denver with no rest.

He ate his routine breakfast of canned peaches, confirming at least a rifle and a shotgun were loaded before hitting the road. He spent last night studying the map of the area, learning the best route to take to the airport.

Robert turned on the car and left Larkwood behind, hoping the others would remain in place until he returned with Gavin, who might have learned something about their presence in the city.

He had woken with the sun, eager to have as many hours in the day ahead of him, not knowing how long it would take to venture around the airport grounds. It was a massive space, and while they understood the logistics of an underground world, neither Robert or Gavin had any clue how to access it.

"Nothing to worry about," Robert told himself as he reached the freeway. "He's had plenty of time to find it."

He only had to slow down for a couple of toppled over semi-trucks, the particular stretch of road heavy with commercial traffic. None of the blasts seemed to have affected the inter-states or main highways, and Robert wondered if that had been done intentionally, considering a government truck had already driven this far on its own.

"Nothing the government does is ever by accident," he said.

He shook the thought out of his mind as he approached the airport. A beaming red light caught his attention. As he drove closer, Robert found it was actually a red eye that belonged to a towering statue of a blue horse standing on its hind legs as it overlooked Peña Boulevard.

"What in the hell is that thing?" Robert asked, driving by and unable to look away. The airport and all of its surroundings had been successfully demolished, but this frightening sculpture somehow survived, not so much as a crack in its fiberglass exterior. A chill rushed up his back as he passed, happy to leave it behind.

He rounded a curve and headed for what was once the east terminal, now a massive crater filled with the airport's bones. Robert slowed the car down and stopped on the side of the road, hesitant to continue any further as he spotted an end of the road ahead.

"They attacked this airport directly," he commented as he stepped away from the car, toward the crater. He had seen some holes blasted in the ground around the bigger cities, but none compared to the size, or amount, of the ones at Denver International Airport. Roughly 100 feet ahead, the road dropped off like a cliff.

Robert walked to the edge, peering down at a black hole, dusty broken concrete the only thing visible. Sweat beaded around his forehead, and he fought the slightest of trembles trying to take over his arms. The reality was staring him right in the eye.

Not a survivor was in sight, the world as silent as it had been since he stepped out of the bunker.

"This has to be a mistake," Robert said, shaking his head. He looked from the bottomless pit to the surrounding space, no clear path to navigate to the other side. "Can anybody hear me?"

His voice echoed in many directions. His eyes welled with tears, fists clenching and turning red at his sides. "No, no, no. Everyone was *supposed* to be here. Gavin, can you hear me?!" Robert shouted as loud as he could, a distant caw of a crow the only response.

Robert had grown to believe all of his conspiracy theories, seeing as the biggest one of all turned out to be true, but that didn't mean they were all intertwined. The underground world at this site had been a longstanding theory, one that dated back to the construction of the airport. But here he stood, not a sign of life in the underground. Just miles of the same destruction he had already grown used to seeing.

What if this is part of it? he wondered. *They could have formed this giant crater on purpose, so that it guaranteed those underground are left alone. And what about all the tunnels Gavin had mentioned? The ones that led to nowhere, or at least they seemed?*

Robert turned and ran back to the car, falling behind the wheel and turning the engine on in unison. "I don't fucking think so!" he shouted, spinning away from the median and driving west, off the road and into an open field. The crater spanned two miles until he ran into a wall of debris piled like a mountain. He screamed, punching the steering wheel until his fists turned sore.

"This isn't happening," he snarled, panting for breath. No visible path existed that would get him around the crater. His only option to confirm an underground world was to drive off the cliff and find out for himself. He hadn't quite lost his grip on reality to do such a thing, but turned the car around and drove back for another look.

Relax, he thought. *Go to Gavin's apartment and see if he's there. He's too smart to have not left you some sort of clue.*

Disgusted, Robert turned away from the airport and drove back the way he had come, headed for the ruins of downtown Denver.

"These government assholes are gonna pay for this," Robert growled as he floored the accelerator. "I know that world is down there—and they're going to let me in if it's the last thing they do."

"Oh, Dad, none of that is true," Gavin's voice said, causing

Robert to gasp and slam the brakes, spinning out of control as he caught a glimpse of his son in the passenger seat. The car came to a halt inches away from a battered, concrete median wall.

"This isn't happening," Robert said, looking down at his lap and shaking his head. "Not again, none of this is real."

He forced his head up toward the passenger seat, willing his mind to not see the illusion of his son. But Gavin remained, leaning back in the seat, dressed in his usual attire of athletic pants and a baggy hoodie, a ball cap slightly tipped to the right, his shaggy hair protruding from beneath it.

"It's all real, Dad," Gavin said. "I'm dead—just like Mom. She wanted me to tell you hello again, she was too worried what you might do if you saw her again."

Robert snorted. "And seeing *you* here is supposed to help my sanity?"

"I'm sorry to say, Dad, but your sanity hasn't been in the best shape since Mom died. You've been a mental breakdown long in the making. I worried when I left for college, leaving you all alone, but you had the store to keep you busy. These last few weeks in isolation have only left you the time to accept the loss of Mom."

"That's not true," Robert said, meeting his son's light brown eyes. They had the same sort of glow as his wife's when her spirit visited him days earlier. "I've come to terms with all of this many years ago."

"No, you've distracted from the fact. Now that you've been truly alone with nothing to do, the reality is setting in, and you're not okay."

Hearing these words was an emotional jab in the chest, his heart suddenly hollow, Robert on the verge of a heavy cry.

"I've learned to be alone," Robert said, gaining some of his composure. "It hurts sometimes, but it's like a disease, you learn how to live with it."

"I love you, Dad," Gavin said. "I wanted to make sure you knew that. One last time."

"You were supposed to be here, at the airport. That was our plan." A tinge of anger floated into Robert's voice.

"I know. We were wrong. *I* was wrong. I spent so much time trying to look for secret doors and pathways in that airport, and there were so many I found that made no sense. But here we are, and I never found a single piece of actual evidence for the secret underground society. I don't doubt it exists somewhere, but it isn't here."

Tears ran down Robert's face, his face scrunched like it was wringing out every drop in his soul. "You didn't have to die, son. If you couldn't find anything, you should've said so. Adjusting plans was no problem."

Gavin shrugged it off. "I believed in it right until the whole building collapsed. Have you ever been in a dome of death? It's quite interesting looking around, watching the sheer panic on people's faces who know they have no way of surviving. It's one of the more intimate moments I've had, nothing like it."

Robert's throat swelled, the tears no longer streams, but rather a torrent of liquid pouring from his eyes.

"I have to go, Dad, and I only hope that you can learn from this lesson. Find safety and wait for this to blow over. There isn't anyone waiting for you. Do what you must to survive."

Gavin reached over and slapped his father on the back, jolting Robert's head forward, enough for him to no longer see his son when he looked back up.

Robert would heed the advice from his late son, but not until he tended to a matter first. He stared in the rearview, his eyes puffy and bloodshot, crazed like a madman. "I'm going to kill these government assholes."

24

Chapter 24

"I found it all," Ortiz cried out, a hint of rare childish excitement lurking within his voice. He pored over the documents, eyes wide, while he shook his head. "It was only a matter of time, but here it is—all the secrets we need to know."

Camille hurried over. "What do we have?"

"Looks like Susan was working to convert an Exall completely to a human. She seemed to have growing confidence that a breakthrough loomed."

"That's why she kept Sandra down here. Do you think Griffins knew about this?"

"He didn't," Kyle chimed in, handcuffed in the corner. "When I told him of all this, moments before he died, he was completely surprised. My grandma pulled this off without a soul knowing about it."

"None of that is relevant," Ortiz said. "Let's not dwell on what might have been, and focus on what's in front of us."

"Well, don't keep us waiting, Major," Bernard said. "What are we dealing with?"

"Our very own Kyle Wells was injected with Exall blood at

the age of three," Ortiz said, waving the file in the air. "By this point in time, Susan had run enough experiments on herself to feel comfortable taking this gamble. She had every detail worked out to determine the precise amount to inject, knowing she wouldn't have the chance to explain what she had done until much later in Kyle's life."

"So these files were some sort of backup plan in case she died?" Camille asked.

"She says exactly that. In fact, *every* file in that laboratory is backup data for her studies that she had planned to one day deliver to the president. It appears she wanted to work with Kyle in private to get a feel for the full range of his abilities before writing her conclusions and presenting the possibility of delivering this new ability to all the Crew."

"So it's left for us to figure out?"

"Well, it's figured out. She noted that the injection worked successfully and listed the abilities Kyle *should* have. She included instructions for what Kyle needs to do to confirm these abilities."

"What am I supposed to do?" Kyle asked, leaning forward as he stood on his knees in his own corner.

"Telepathy and being able to enter the mind of Exalls around you. That's some heavy stuff, but she seems confident."

Kyle's stomach churned at the thought of entering an Exall's mind. He had learned how the alien species could perform that same act upon humans, but had never heard of it being used the other way around—surely none of them had. It became clear just exactly what Kyle's role was in this grand mission to save and revive the world, and he didn't like it one bit.

"You're not actually thinking of going through with this, are you?" Travis asked Ortiz. "My mom dedicated her entire life to this project, by the sound of it, and I don't see where you have the right to continue it and draw your own conclusions."

"While I agree with you, Mr. Wells, the fact is your mother isn't here to continue her work—and it needs to be completed, especially if these abilities turn out to be true. We'd forever have an advantage over any Exall. If anyone is cut out to meet this challenge, it's the people in this room."

They fell silent for a moment, everyone looking around at each other, weighing their trust with those in the room. Kyle's heart raced, distant within his own chest, as he questioned everything about his life. Had he ever truly been in control of anything, or had his grandmother tried controlling him through Sandra, like a twisted puppeteer? It sounded absurd, but here they were, about to poke his psyche in this continued experiment. And should they find he could enter the minds of Exalls, what did that mean for him? Was the ability recip- rocated by their alien foes? As was normal in the Crew, one answer always led to a dozen more questions.

"What do you think, Ky?" Travis asked, eyebrows cocked.

All heads turned toward him, virtual spotlights as he knelt, handcuffed in the corner like a child in timeout.

"I'm still trying to process all of this. The thought of Exall blood pumping through my veins, for my entire life . . . it's disturbing. My initial thought was to get this blood out of me, but I also trust my grandma and know she wouldn't have left me in a dangerous situation. I don't think me objecting does anything productive—the writing is already on the wall. I have no choice."

"You don't have to do anything you're not comfortable with," Ortiz assured him. "And neither will we. We can tread carefully as we go deeper into these notes, but she left us a pretty clear outline for what to do next."

"And what is that exactly?" Kyle asked.

"Telepathic communication with Sandra—and it looks like we're already set up for it because she specifically says you should be in this room, not the laboratory, to ensure the best results. Are you ready to try it?"

Kyle puffed out his cheeks and blew out a long breath. "Okay, let's see what I've got."

Ortiz stood up, stretching as his back cracked before returning his attention to the binder in his hand. He tore out a piece of paper and handed it to Bernard. "You need to go in the lab and tell Sandra to listen for Kyle trying to communicate with her. Have her repeat what he says and write it down. I have the list of words that Kyle will try to communicate, and we'll compare notes afterward."

"Oooh, alien telephone," Bernard cackled. "Sounds like fun."

He had inched back to his normal self, and everyone clearly appreciated it as they offered laughs of their own. Bernard clicked his pen and snatched the paper from Ortiz without another word, disappearing into the dark hallway, no longer afraid of Sandra.

Ortiz turned to Kyle, eyes narrowing on him. "Okay, Wells, now you're up. According to these notes, the initial time you use this ability is more like a deep meditation. I hope you did well in the psychological courses we ran you through for training."

Kyle nodded. The courses had included a wide range of lessons, from learning about the psychological effects of life as a Crew member, all the way to blocking an Exall from entering your mind. Somewhere in the midst was a class on meditation, and how to use it should you find yourself mentally overtaken by an Exall.

"I need the rest of you to be silent," Ortiz said to Camille and Travis. He stepped toward the ladder and flicked the light switch down, leaving them in pure blackness. "Kyle, you can either lie down or stay seated, just find which position is more comfortable."

Kyle obliged, opting to lie flat on his back, resting his cuffed hands atop his stomach. "I'm set."

"Okay, close your eyes, draw in deep breaths while counting to five, then exhale through your mouth using the same count. Keep that breathing cycle going while you tense your body from toes to head. Keep your mental focus on your breathing—now tense your toes, and release when you exhale. Do this all the way up your body, moving in sections. Shins and calves next."

Kyle did as instructed, letting the darkness consume him, silencing the distant sound of his father and Camille breathing, drifting into a world of his own, finding a sweet spot of isolation. Over the next two minutes, Kyle tensed areas of his body as narrated by Major Ortiz, the deep baritone of his voice also moving into the background of his focus. Once Ortiz guided him around his own body, he changed instructions to have Kyle focus on his surroundings. He maintained his steady, deep breathing, now letting the smells waft into his nose, ears focused on the faintest of sounds within the vicinity.

What felt like a tunnel flowed from Kyle's head, an invisible pathway that he watched with his mind, rising and bending around the corner where the hallway waited. While he couldn't see where the other end had gone, he could sense it, the sounds and smells changing to those of the laboratory with its soft humming of machines and musty stench after a few years of abandonment. That's when his head thudded slightly forward, his invisible tunnel running into what felt like a wall.

Hello, Kyle, Sandra said, her voice clear and loud, but only within his mind.

"I'm in," Kyle mumbled to Ortiz, keeping the rest of his concentration on the open line of communication with the alien in the other room. He had no idea how fragile this tunnel was. Could a flick of the light switch make it collapse? He didn't want to find out at the moment, but they would need a deeper understanding of how this ability truly functioned.

"Okay," Ortiz said, his voice still floating in a different dimension. "Five words. Say them to Sandra—nothing else. Pentagon. Easter. Beach. Mountain. Cactus."

Ortiz repeated this series of words two more times, but Kyle had what he needed.

Pentagon. Easter. Beach. Mountain. Cactus.

Kyle thought these words and trusted they would carry through the tunnel and into Sandra's mind. He waited for thirty seconds after hearing nothing back, and was about to think the words again, but she finally responded.

I've passed the words along, Kyle. Isn't this fun? Your grandmother and I would sit in this tunnel all day and talk. I don't know what they're telling you, but remember that this ability—and all the ones we have—works much like human muscles. If you exercise them enough, they'll become stronger and bigger. You'll also not need to try as hard to open up this tunnel. Susan used to quilt an entire blanket while we carried on our conversation.

"Wells!" Ortiz said in an elevated voice. It momentarily broke his concentration, but the tunnel remained in place, and he kept his eyes closed, wanting to chat more with Sandra.

So, we can just hop into this . . . place whenever we want to talk?

Yes, of course, Sandra replied. *In time, you'll be able to turn it off and on by thinking about it, and will be able to do it even while you converse out loud with others around you.*

Kyle couldn't resist the shaking of his body from Major Ortiz, who had grabbed him around the shoulders and jolted him back to the real world. His eyes shot open, the lights back on and blinding him as he shot his arm up to shield them.

"You okay?" Ortiz asked, still squatting over Kyle. "Sorry about that, you weren't responding, and we're not sure what exactly we're dealing with here."

Kyle sat up and shook his head. "Nothing to worry about. I think it worked. She heard the words from me, and I heard her respond."

"Did she say anything in particular?"

"No, just confirmation that she heard me."

Kyle's stomach tightened from the lie. He wasn't sure why he felt the need to hide the truth. Perhaps he was still trying to come to terms with the reality of the matter, or maybe the thought of having a full conversation with someone in a different room, without opening his lips, was too intimidating to admit.

Bernard strolled back into the room, a slip of paper clutched in his grip. His eyes met Kyle's, prompting a brief grin before handing the paper over to Ortiz.

The Major looked it over, smiling. "Looks like we're in business, folks. Exact match for the words."

Camille worked her way over. "What does that mean? What's next?"

Ortiz folded the paper and slipped it into the file. "It means we're staying here longer. I'll admit, I was skeptical—this all seemed like a long-shot, but this is further proof that Susan might have known more than the Crew. Think about what she pulled off with this. If any of us tried something like this and were caught, we'd be shot dead in our homes. Not only did she give Kyle this unique ability, she kept it a secret for her entire career. She had to have known the risk she was taking all along."

"Does this mean I can get out of these handcuffs?" Kyle asked, Travis nodding in agreement.

"I want to read a couple other files first before making that call. There's still a lot we don't understand, and we can't afford any risk. On that note, let's buckle in and get to work. We have more to test with Wells, and I came across some interesting studies on our Exall friend to look at. Let's keep doing what we've been with reading through these files."

Camille and Bernard nodded and returned to their corners, leaving Kyle to look over to his father, locking eyes with him and wishing he could communicate with him instead of Sandra.

25

Chapter 25

Six hours later, Kyle sat in his corner, no longer handcuffed.

Ortiz had disappeared into the lab for nearly the entire time, digging through the file cabinets, splaying sheets of paper across the floor and countertops. He arrived back at the bunker with a stern expression on his face. "We have a very interesting opportunity in front of us. It's risky, but the reward can change the world forever."

Everyone put down the files they were working on and shifted their attention to the major.

"Susan was working on a special injection. A cure, I suppose you could call it. Sandra might actually be a little more human than we thought. Seeing as she's been the only test subject for Susan, it's safe to assume that some of her DNA has been transitioned toward that of a human."

"This would mean no more Exalls," Camille said, more to herself as she pressed a finger to her lips. "Forever."

"Precisely. This would be the ultimate weapon. We can't say for sure if a day will come when there are no more Exalls, but imagine if we had a way of stripping them of their abilities, leaving them to fight us on a level playing field. I know our organization would have no problem defeating them in that scenario."

"How close was she to figuring this out?" Bernard asked.

"According to her notes, very close. This was actually the last thing she was working on, by the looks of it. Her attention got diverted away once the Exalls started arriving in Colorado, otherwise I think she may have sealed the deal."

"Then we have to finish it," Travis said, joining the small circle that had formed around Ortiz. "I know I don't have any say in Crew matters, but if my mom was this close to ending the threat of this species, wouldn't you want that?"

"I agree," Kyle added, a soft grin on his face. "I don't think it's a matter of her experiment working or not, but rather *when* she'd get it all together. There are five of us here who can figure this out—the odds are in our favor."

"Sounds like everyone is on board," Ortiz said, satisfied. "It sounds like a pretty straightforward process from what I've read... involves some poking of the Exall, but she won't feel it, as they have a resistance to pain. Apparently, all we need to do is tinker with some ingredients and chemicals, inject the mixture into Sandra, then wait an hour before drawing some of her blood and running it through her diagnostics machine. Susan outlined the precise results we should look for to know if it's working, or how we should continue testing."

"Sounds like a longer process than I thought," Bernard said. "We have to wait an hour in between each test? This could take days."

"It could, but don't you think even a week is worth it? If we find this, then figure a way to mass produce it, we can go back into the world with no fear."

"Except for one thing, Major—the Exalls aren't going to just sign up to get this injection. Are you suggesting we just go around stabbing them all with needles, and hope we don't get killed in the process?"

"Of course not. We'd work to get the liquid placed in the choker bullets. I'm familiar with the process of how they were made at our lab in D.C. We would just insert this new liquid instead of the one currently in use. Then, we'd just have to shoot the Exalls, only this time they won't die—they'll transform into humans."

"Am I the only one thinking through all the possibilities and consequences?" Bernard asked, a tinge of anger surfacing. "Let's say we shoot fifty Exalls with this magic medicine, then what? We wait for them to become human and kill them? Welcome them into our new society? Let them colonize their own country? What exactly is our goal with this?"

"We don't know. Susan didn't know either. This is a matter of reducing the threat they pose to us, then figuring it out from there. Maybe some will be good, some will be bad—just like they've always been. We'll just have to see and decide based on how they react."

Bernard tossed his hands in the air, grabbing the sides of his head. "Are you listening to yourself, Major? You want to go through all this work just to see what *might* happen? Gamble with our lives? What if it ends up turning them all into murderous zombies a month down the road, then what? This seems like a very unnecessary gamble to take when our focus needs to be on rebuilding this country, as instructed. We can just keep shooting them dead as we've always done."

"What's the point in rebuilding if the threat still looms?" Major Ortiz asked calmly. "I understand your points, but you need to consider it from my angle. We can rebuild in a few years, maybe even have a whole new society up and running with whatever survivors we can find. But we'll always be on the defense. Sure, we may not know now what we plan on doing with any converted Exalls, but at least we won't have to worry about having our brains hijacked. I see this more as a long-term solution."

"Well, I vote against doing this. Kyle has his new ability—we should take it and run, finish the job we set out to do."

"And we will, as soon as we do this," Ortiz said. "And this isn't up for a vote—this is a command that we will see this experiment through."

Bernard shook his head, turning away from the group and returning to his corner to cool off. Kyle caught a quick glimpse of his face and thought Bernard might throw a punch if he hadn't stepped away.

"Let's head into the lab and get to work," Ortiz continued to the rest of the group. "Franzen, take some time to gather your thoughts, and please join us. This is still a team effort, mind you."

The major pivoted and led them into the dark hallway, his steps sounding heavier than usual, perhaps fighting off some pent up rage of his own. Seconds later they entered the laboratory, Sandra rolling her head to greet them.

"Hello, all," she said in a gentle voice.

"Sandra, do you recall any of the injections that Susan had been giving to you?" Ortiz asked, stepping up to her. "Did they make you feel any particular way? Have any effects?"

"I remember," she replied. "I know she was trying to change me into a human, but I never felt different after any of the shots."

"Her notes show you received around twenty different shots over the course of a few months. Not one had any effect?"

"No. I suppose our bodies are built to fight off any foreign objects entering it. She didn't speak to me in much detail about what each shot was, only that it wouldn't kill me."

"Dammit," Ortiz muttered under his breath. "Okay, team, let's get to work. Wells—both of you—I want you to work on the next creation. All ingredients are in the side cabinets." He nodded in the direction on the other side of Sandra. "Monroe, you and I will work on injecting the next test into Sandra and see what happens. Let's get to it."

They broke into different directions, Kyle and his father crossing the room and rummaging through the cabinets. Travis pulled out handfuls of small bottles with clear liquids, each one with a label identifying the contents within. Kyle recognized many of the elemental names thanks to high school science classes, but had no idea how they were supposed to be used in conjunction with each other. He kept stealing glances over his shoulder to his major and captain, worried about Sandra's safety in the hands of lifelong Crew members. The major stood under the bright lights that shone over the table where the Exall lay, holding up a vial with a syringe inserted into it as he drew out the fluid.

"Commencing test for vial number 324," he said, hovering the needle above Sandra's face. She stared at it calmly, not bothered by the prospect of being poked like a lab rat.

Ortiz lowered the syringe and inserted it into Sandra's left arm, pressing down on the plunger as he gritted his teeth, eyes narrow with focus. He pulled it out and dropped the needle on the small table next to him.

"Now we wait," he said, crossing his arms and taking a step

back, Camille joining by his side.

Sandra remained unbothered on the table, eyes glossy and staring at the ceiling. Kyle looked over again, following her gaze to the light fixture directly above her body, noticing it subtly dim and brighten every couple of seconds. He whipped back around to the counter where he was organizing the bottles of fluids and closed his eyes to focus on his breathing and the still silence around him. He had no idea if Travis was paying him any attention, but had to open up the tunnel again with Sandra.

After a minute of effort, the free-floating sensation of entering this third dimension filled all of Kyle's senses. *What are you doing?* he asked, slowly opening his eyes to test the waters of carrying this conversation while still appearing hard at work. He opened them all the way without disruption to the tunnel. *Sandra, can you hear me?*

She didn't respond after a minute of multiple attempts to contact her, so Kyle wondered if the tunnel wasn't actually functioning, or if she was simply ignoring him. He felt he had a firm grasp on his new mental ability, and spun around for a direct view of the Exall. Ortiz and Camille stood in their same places, studying Sandra, oblivious to the flickering light above.

A slight rumble came from below their feet, as if a train had just blown by the house. Sandra shrieked, a deafening sound that bounced around the room like a bat trying to find its way out.

Travis swiveled around to join everyone else who was already gawking at her. Sandra's teeth clenched, like she was fake smiling, but what caught all of their attention was her arms and legs bulging with muscles that seemed to have grown in the past few seconds. The harnesses strapped around her limbs and torso stretched, and no one thought the metal clasps that kept them secured would actually give out.

With a powerful bellow, Sandra's eyes bulged out of her face as she flexed her limbs even more, now clearly trying to escape the restraint as she pulled the harnesses away from the table. The ground rumbled again, this time with enough force to knock everyone off their feet, sending the Crew members and Travis to the floor, as they scrambled to regain their footing.

The clasps popped off the harness, shooting in every direction like miniature missiles.

"Shoot her!" Ortiz shouted, but his words were mostly drowned out by Sandra howling. "Shoot her now!"

Kyle, in shock, realized his tunnel was still open. *Sandra, why are you doing this?*

She spun around and locked eyes with his gaze. *I've been waiting for this moment—have been told for a long time that it would come. One day the humans would have their last hope to save their species—it's my job to exterminate them.*

Kyle's hands patted around his waist in search of his pistol, but he had left it in his bag in the bunker, assuming he was safe underground with an Exall who had never once shown the ability to harm so much as a butterfly. His mind spun with confusion, wondering how much was true. Did Sandra really live in this laboratory for multiple decades, just to deliver the final nail in the coffin? Did she actually pretend to befriend his grandmother for all that time, learning about Susan's family and friends, the intricacies of her life? But more importantly, did she actually think she could get away with this? Having four Crew members in the same vicinity seemed a sure bet for losing, but Exalls weren't known for playing the odds.

Sandra snarled at Kyle like a rabid dog and lunged over the

table, gliding through the air with the ease of a rabbit. Kyle crouched and swung up his arms to shield his head, unaware his father had taken a leap at the same time, tackling the Exall in midair, bringing them both down to the ground in a messy crash.

Travis had landed on top of her and immediately wrestled away from her flailing hands, kicking her in the jaw as he scooted back toward Kyle.

"Dad!" Kyle shouted, but all attention remained on Sandra, slowly rising to her feet.

"Get down!" Bernard shouted from the doorway, and everyone obliged, jumping out of the way of his pistol's pathway.

With a quick shot, Sandra caught a slug square in the forehead, black, tarry blood promptly oozing from the wound. Her head bobbed from side to side as she stumbled like a drunk leaving the bar. She grinned, catching her balance on the counter behind her. "You're not going to make it. There are so many more of us—humans have no chance."

With those last words, Sandra collapsed to the ground with a heavy thud, and everyone gathered around to watch in amazement as her body disintegrated before their eyes. The muscles she had just grown deflated, leaving her flesh an oversized sack. Moments later, that same flesh oozed fine streams of smoke, until it all gradually turned into a pile of gray dust.

Bernard shook his head. "I've never seen anything like that before."

Ortiz threw an arm around his shoulder, pulling him in for an embrace. "I don't think many of us have, but all that matters is that you saved us. Thank you."

Bernard had tears welled in his eyes as he nodded. "I'm glad

I stayed back, or we might all be dead."

26

Chapter 26

Less than an hour after shooting Sandra dead in the laboratory, Kyle had stormed out of the room and returned to the bunker, hiding in his corner and bawling tears of sorrow and rage. He understood the need to kill Sandra, but he couldn't help but feel stunned.

Travis revealed Sandra had bitten him on the shoulder during their scuffle, prompting an immediate blood test that showed he had become infected with Exall DNA. Everyone else waited in the lab for Travis's blood results to come back. They spent the time arguing and discussing what the hell had gone so wrong. They debated if they had incorrectly formulated the injection and caused a rabid reaction, or if Sandra had been waiting for the right time to pounce. Kyle figured they'd never find out.

Life became a blur from the moment Ortiz read the results, and that's when Kyle dashed out of the room without a word. He knew what it meant, logistically, to have someone in their group become infected.

Heavy footsteps echoed from the dark hallway, prompting Kyle to wipe away his tears and puff out his chest as he stood tall. Major Ortiz entered the bunker, his shoulders slouched, head slightly hung low.

"How are you holding up, Wells?" he asked in the softest voice he could manage.

Kyle's body trembled beneath his baggy clothes, and he hoped the major didn't notice. He couldn't believe what he was about to attempt against the current highest-ranking person in the American government. His words in the next couple minutes could have dire consequences for everyone in the group, and possibly even for his own life.

"I'm okay," Kyle said, his teeth chattering with nerves. "I just . . ."

He shook his head and broke into a fresh wave of tears, unable to contain his emotions, not confident he could actually stand up to the major.

Ortiz shuffled over and placed his large hands on each of Kyle's shoulders. "I know this is hard, but we have protocol to follow for good reason."

"Oh, you know how it feels to have your father infected by an Exall?! All because he wanted to save your life? Please tell me about your experience."

"Look, Wells, I haven't had that specifically happen, but we've all gone through some shit. I don't have to share your exact experience to feel your pain, so trust me when I tell you I understand."

"We don't have to kill him," Kyle said. "There has to be another way. He's tied down in a room full of medicines that can heal him."

"Those are all meant for use on full-blooded Exalls—we have no idea what effects they might have on your dad."

"Can't be any worse than what just happened." Kyle crossed

his arms to keep them from shaking.

"We can leave him strapped to the table in there, but is that what you really want? If none of us make it to the end of this mission, are you willing to die knowing your father will be buried alive for the rest of eternity?"

"No one else is dying. I'll be damned if any of us get caught without our pistols again." Kyle patted his waistband for assurance.

"No one knows what's going to happen, so we have to plan for all possibilities. And it's about time for us to head out."

"Bullshit! I don't think so. You were ready to stay here for however long it took to figure out this injection, but now you don't want to do the same thing to save my actual father? We're staying."

"Kyle, it's not safe anymore. We need to put your father to rest and keep moving—this portion of the mission has turned into a failure, and that's on me for falling into the trap of complacency. It almost felt like home, and I think that's why no one thought of bringing their guns with them into the lab."

Kyle shook his head. "You can deal with what went wrong, but I'm staying here."

"It's an order for you to finish this mission," Ortiz snapped.

"I'm the one with the ability to talk with these Exalls. You can drag me out of this bunker, but I'll refuse to tell you what I hear from them."

Kyle's stomach tightened like an iron fist was clenching it. His major could flatten him should he desire, and Kyle hoped he'd refrain from such hostility.

"Wells," he said, taking a deep breath, balling his fists. "We are on an official mission from the United States government. Your father has been infected and will soon become an Exall.

We have to put him down. Then, we are moving west to complete the rest of the mission. There is no bargaining on this matter—it is an order. Should you choose to not comply, I will hold you in contempt of the Crew, an act that is punishable anywhere from forty years in a private, Crew-operated prison, all the way up to the penalty of death. Do you understand?"

His eyes blazed into Kyle, causing the teenager to gulp the ball of spit that had pooled in the back of his mouth. Both his and his father's life teetered in the balance, so he took a moment to process all possibilities. They held their standoff for two entire minutes, Ortiz not breaking eye contact, while Kyle stared at the floor in deep thought.

"If I recall, Major, there is a section in the official Crew handbook that addresses this matter—I believe it was Section Four, so correct me if I'm wrong. But it states that any Crew member held in contempt by a superior must stand trial to a panel of fellow members chosen by the Colonel. It also states that, unless the member in question has caused any direct harm to a colleague, then they may work as normal, free of restraint, until the trial begins. You are not the Colonel, and we do not have a panel. Hold me in contempt if you must, but I'll be staying here, as allowed by our laws."

Ortiz opened his mouth to speak, closed it back up, and crossed his arms while shaking his head. His pursed lips turned into a smirk. "Impressive, Wells. Not many people can quote our handbook like scripture—I don't even know all the rules in there by memory."

"Sorry, Major, I didn't mean to show you up. I just remember this one because I found it odd that it even needed to be mentioned. Everything I had gathered about the Crew suggested nothing like that could ever happen. I asked Colonel Griffins about it, and he insisted I keep that rule handy. He told me this was still the military, and someone my age might get pushed around by superiors."

Ortiz nodded. "Oh, Colonel Griffins, rest his soul. I guess he's still here helping you. Okay, Wells, I'll make you a deal. We can stay here another week and see if we can't find something that can reverse the course for your dad. It's still early, and he's not showing any symptoms, so we have the leeway to work on it. But, we can't stay here forever. That week timeline is solid, you understand? And if we can't get your dad fixed up, we can take him with us, in restraints, so long as he's still not showing any signs of becoming a full-on Exall."

"And if he *does* show symptoms?"

Ortiz pinched his lips and shrugged. "You know what we have to do. I'm sorry."

Kyle gathered his thoughts, making sure he wasn't leaving any possible leverage untouched. "Okay, deal," he said, sticking out a hand to shake.

Ortiz grabbed it. "I'm sorry this got so out of control. We're all on edge after what happened, and now this. No one wants to kill your father, trust me, but no one wants to end up like him, either. This is a sticky situation, and it's my job to guide us through it as safely as possible."

"I know, Major. Thank you for working with me."

"Let's keep this between me and you. I'll tell everyone the new plan, but no need for them to know how you threw the book at me—the last thing we need is Franzen memorizing his handbook to pull out a technicality for everything we do."

They both shared a laugh over this. "Will do, Major."

"Perfect. Now, you stay here a few minutes, get yourself together, and come back to the lab so we can get started on helping Travis."

Ortiz slapped Kyle on the shoulder before turning back down the hallway. Kyle slunk into his chair, grateful to have survived the tense encounter, worried sick of what would happen if they couldn't cleanse his father of the Exall blood now flowing through his veins.

27

Chapter 27

Kyle had taken at least ninety minutes to fall asleep, by his count, tossing and turning while he thought of his father strapped to the table in the laboratory, just as Sandra had been. They weren't able to make any meaningful strides before calling it a night, Ortiz opting for a night of rest to tackle a full day tomorrow where they would dedicate their time to helping Travis.

Even as he slept, it was light, the steady snoring from Bernard sure to keep him distracted throughout the night. It wasn't until the whispers started that brought him all the way back to full consciousness.

Kyle, can you hear me? Can you hear me? a voice repeated in his head. He had been sleeping and had no tunnel open, but the sensation felt as if the voices were knocking on its door. Kyle focused on the surrounding sounds, wanting to make sure it wasn't one of his colleagues calling out for him in the night.

Everyone around him remained asleep, so he lay back and focused on opening the tunnel, the voice growing from an inaudible whisper to the regular tone of his father.

Kyle, it's me.

Dad? How did you—

I don't know. I've just been laying here this whole time. I've heard other voices. I think something bad is coming.

Kyle scanned the room, confirming that no one had woken. *Okay, slow down. Were the voices from other Exalls?*

I think so. I didn't recognize any, and they were talking about gathering to 'finish the job.'

What did you say back?

Nothing. They weren't even talking to me directly, at least not from what I could tell. It was like overhearing a conversation in another room.

Kyle became dizzy. The last thing he needed was a secret like this to keep from Ortiz. If word leaked to the major that Travis was in any sort of contact with outside Exalls, it may very well lead to him being restrained for the rest of his time on Earth. Or worse.

When did you hear this conversation? Kyle asked.

About an hour ago. After it ended, I started trying to reach out to you. I have no idea how any of this works—was only hoping that you'd actually hear me.

We can't tell anyone about this. Not about the conversation you heard, or even about you and me communicating in this way. They'll lock us both up until we get back to D.C.

Don't worry about me, I'm not saying a damn thing.

How are you doing? I've just wanted a moment in private to talk, but I guess this will have to do.

This is kind of cool, I suppose. I feel okay. I haven't had any desire for food, water, or sleep since the attack, but I'm sure that's just the shock that hasn't worn off yet.

Kyle knew the truth of Exalls not requiring any sort of human necessities, but kept his mouth shut for now. *I'm sure it'll all be back in the morning. But you haven't been feeling any sort of evil thoughts? Or like a helplessness to keep from lashing out?*

Wow, is that what I have to look forward to? I haven't felt anything like that yet.

Not necessarily, but it is possible—the effects can range all across the board.

I love you, Ky. Hope you know that. None of us know how this is going to play out, so I wanted to tell you now, just in case.

Dad, don't talk like that. We can get you back to normal.

Kyle knew there were no guarantees, but hadn't yet confronted the reality of all outcomes, at least not the darker ones.

I'm going to do my best for what I can control, Travis said. *I don't know how any of it works, but I'm not going to just stand by if they try to take over my mind. And any information I hear will be relayed straight to you.*

Just make sure you don't communicate with me while anyone is examining you. I don't exactly know what all they can tell about your thoughts.

Of course. And you should let me know if there's anything I can do to help, even if it's just to keep an ear out for these others.

Kyle's head tightened, the tunnel seeming to swell, other voices chattering in the distance.

Do you hear that? Travis asked. *I think it's the same ones from earlier.*

Don't say a word. Stay quiet until they're gone.

Kyle sat up, suddenly wondering if the Exalls had a way of harming within this odd void. He figured nothing physical could befall him, but wanted to remain in hiding as much as possible.

The voice grew louder, approaching.

Larkwood, Colorado. You know this place. Our boys had a lot of fun here a few years ago. The school we attacked was just over there.

Ahhh, yes, said another voice, also deep and raspy. *And we haven't spotted any others around the country?*

We handled a group in Washington on the first day. We have eyes on another group in Texas, and should wipe out a third in Minneapolis.

Perfect, that's what I love hearing. If there are truly none of them left to shoot us, the land is ours for the taking.

Indeed, it is. We should be proud. Things fell into place and we were able to capitalize. I guess centuries of patience have paid off.

What about the boy? The evil woman's grandchild.

He's nothing special—we'll take him out just as easily as any of them.

Kyle had to control his breathing from snowballing into hyperventilation. He remained silent, hoping that was enough to stay concealed within the tunnel.

If anything, we'll save him for last. A ceremonial ending to our efforts. That Wells woman took so much from us, it's only fitting her spawn be the final life we take before ruling the land.

They made it difficult for us to rebuild—burned everything down.

It will be fine, and look at the bright side—we get to start from scratch, really mold this land the way we want. The humans had no reason for where they placed cities, and they left so much open land. Thousands of miles of nothing. We will be much more efficient in how we allocate our resources.

I suppose you're right. Well, we should probably head back and set up camp. Who knows how long it will be until they show their faces?

Doesn't matter to me, because if they don't show up by tomorrow night, then all of us will start sifting through the remains of this town until we find them.

The two shared a laugh before the voices trailed off, back into the distance. Kyle promptly returned to his regular consciousness, closing the tunnel with his father, not wanting to take any risk.

"How did I hear them?" he whispered to himself, wanting to feel words leave his lips. From his understanding, the tunnel ability had a range, one which he didn't know. It struck him, as sudden as a punch to the throat, that the Exalls were in the immediate area. "The school was just over there," he repeated the Exalls' words.

Kyle lay back down, staring at the ceiling, realizing the aliens were most likely standing just above them. His only question now was if they knew Kyle and his team were below. Their conversation could have been a mere taunt, a flexing of their muscle to prove to Kyle that he and the Crew had no chance of completing their mission to restore the country. He held his gaze to the ceiling, trying to picture the outside world, two Exalls roaming the tattered remains of his hometown.

They're here.

28

Chapter 28

Kyle didn't sleep the rest of the night, exhausted by the time everyone else woke up. *Why is it impossible to sleep before encountering the Exalls?* he thought.

During the rest of the night, he changed his mind at least fifty times regarding whether to tell Major Ortiz about the conversation he overheard. Having plenty of free time, he considered every angle of the decision, figuring how either way would affect them both as a group, and as individuals. He ultimately decided to tell the major, and now squirmed as he watched Ortiz get ready for the day ahead, oblivious that whatever plans he had were about to be ruined.

Camille slipped into the dark hallway to change clothes, leaving the bunker as an unofficial men's locker room for a quick five minutes.

"Good morning, gentlemen," Ortiz said to Kyle and Bernard while he slipped into his boots. "How was your night?"

"These sleeping pills are the only thing keeping me sane," Bernard said. "Without them, I might be going on a week without sleep."

Ortiz chuckled. "How about you, Wells—did you manage any peace last night?"

Kyle squirmed, struggling to find the best positioning for his feet. "Actually, Major, something happened last night that I need to tell you about."

The seriousness in his voice grabbed both men's attention. Camille entered the bunker, immediately noticing a shift in the mood. "What's going on?" she asked, looking to Ortiz for answers.

"There were Exalls here last night," Kyle said. "I heard them talking."

"Excuse me?" Ortiz snatched the pistol from his bed and cocked it, prompting Kyle to raise his hands in a relaxing gesture.

"Not in here, Major. They were outside. Above ground."

"How do you know?"

"I heard them in my head."

"You sure it wasn't a dream?" Bernard asked. "I know I've had plenty of nightmares with the bastards."

Kyle shook his head. "I was awake, and very aware. It was the same sensation as when I communicated with Sandra, only this time it felt like eavesdropping on a conversation I wasn't supposed to hear."

"Dammit," Ortiz snarled. "This is the price we pay for staying in one spot too long. This is on me."

"No, it's not, Major," Camille snapped back. "We all agreed to stay here, so don't even try to take the blame. Besides, this was bound to happen on this mission. Did you really think we'd make it across the entire country and back without meeting some sort of resistance from them?"

Ortiz crossed his arms. "What did they say, Wells?"

"I didn't get to hear the entire conversation. I think they started too far out of my range. But once they were close, I definitely heard them talking about us. They know we're in this city, and there are more of them coming to hunt us down."

"Major, what are we supposed to do?!" Bernard cried. "We're sitting ducks down here."

"There were only two of them in this conversation?" Ortiz asked.

"Correct."

"We can work with this, team. Let's calm down and focus on a game plan. We can confront them today and wipe them out. We still have them outnumbered. Then we have to get back on the road and out of here before any others show up. Thoughts?"

"I'm not leaving my dad," Kyle said.

"I know—and we will figure out how to best transport him with us—safely."

"We need to hit them as soon as possible," Camille said. "And it will be to our advantage to get them in the daylight. Think we can whip up something in the next two hours?"

"This team can do anything," Ortiz said.

Kyle's stomach dropped. He had expected a reaction like this, but had no idea it would move so quickly.

"There's not much we can do for preparation," Ortiz contin-ued. "We have no idea what's going on outside. Best we can do is devise a protection scheme. I think Wells should remain safe and try to listen for them, and relay us any information. And the three of us can work in a triangle with our backs to each other, that way all angles are covered and we can react as needed."

"Should we bring the bombs?" Bernard asked. He had

been tasked with packing all weaponry for the trip. One of his pet projects was the creation of explosives made of the same substance that went into choker bullets. It was still in the testing phase and never received final approval from the Crew, but with no one to say otherwise, he brought them along, calculating that they could wipe out around one hundred Exalls per bomb, if gathered closely together. Ortiz had applauded the advancement and insisted Bernard bring all the bombs he had created—ten of them—on this mission.

"Let's bring a couple, just in case, but it doesn't sound like we'll be needing that much firepower. Hopefully, this is a quick encounter."

"It's never simple with these monsters," Camille said, stuffing two additional magazines of choker bullets into her backpack. "Look at the two soldiers we lost in Michigan—they outnumbered the one Exall in the middle of nowhere and neither made it home. We shouldn't feel any sort of advantage."

"She's right," Ortiz said. "I know we've all felt more relaxed since leaving D.C. and spending so much time on the open road, but the threat remains the same as it always was. Let's not forget what we just witnessed last night with Travis and Sandra."

"Have you checked on your dad yet, Wells?"

The question turned up the dials on Kyle's adrenaline, hoping no guilt would shine through. He figured if any of them were to propose the idea of Travis being able to communicate telepathically, it would be Bernard. So he avoided eye contact with him and focused on the major.

"I haven't yet this morning. I can go check on him now."

Ortiz held up a hand. "We need to finalize what we're going to do first. And maybe mention this to your dad since he might have the same ability to hear other Exalls. Perhaps he picked up other parts of the conversation you had missed."

"Good idea," Kyle said, mustering all the confidence he could behind his voice.

"We might even want to bring him with us," Bernard added. "I know he's not a formal Crew member, but I understand he has the training of one thanks to his mother. He can handle a gun, right?"

Kyle nodded.

"Maybe he and Kyle can be the two who stay close by while we hunt these Exalls down."

Kyle's head throbbed with the sensation from last night, someone knocking on his mental door to the tunnel. No one in the bunker appeared to notice him rub his head in discomfort, so he concentrated on answering the call.

"I need some water," Kyle muttered, turning away from the group and returning to his corner, where he fished a bottle of water out of his stash of goods. He sat down and drank from it, mind focused on opening the tunnel.

Once seated, his mind relaxed enough to allow Travis to be heard. *Kyle! Are you okay? What's going on out there?*

I told everyone about the visitors we had last night—I didn't tell them about you. I might have to run if they start talking to me again, just so you know.

What did they say?

They're planning to go outside and hunt them down, then leave Larkwood. I told them I'm not going anywhere without you.

That's nice of you, Ky, but not necessary. Do whatever is needed to finish this mission. If I have to wait down here for a little while, it makes no difference to me—I was down here anyway. Now it seems I won't have to worry about eating or sleeping, so just add some more boredom to the list.

No—I won't allow it. We are also talking about bringing you with us. They might ask you about any new abilities you have—still don't mention anything, pretend like you're feeling normal. I don't trust what they'll do if you start showing more symptoms.

I'm afraid it's too late, Ky. I have a small gray patch forming on my forearm. I've been bored and only have so much to look at being tied down. I noticed it last night, but thought I just might have been seeing things. It's still there, and I think it got a little bigger.

Jesus Christ, Dad, they'll never let you live if you actually start turning into an Exall.

I know. That's why I said to leave me here. I feel myself changing. It's a gradual process, not even constant. After we talked last night, I had the strongest urge to choke someone. No idea who or why, but I wanted it. Thinking about it made me drool.

How many times has that happened?

Only twice. I feel like I still have decent control over my emotions, but those two instances ramped up out of my control.

This rage can be good if you can channel it. You can be helpful fighting off the other Exalls. I'm just trying to think of selling points to get you outside with us.

I wish I knew how I'd react outside. I like to think I have enough control to not attack you guys, but how can I really trust that?

I don't know. We can figure it out. I should get going now, been in here a while.

Okay, I'll see you soon. And remember, I love you, son. No matter what happens to me, you need to finish this mission. It's bigger than all of us.

Before Kyle could respond, he felt his father leave the mental tunnel, silence filling his head as he stared blankly at the water bottle resting on his lap. The other three had been carrying on a conversation, but didn't appear to have noticed Kyle mentally slip away for a couple of minutes. He stood up to rejoin them.

"We're *all* going outside," Ortiz said. "I want to run a couple tests on your dad's blood, and if all checks out, he'll be joining us too."

"Oh? What changed your mind?"

"The unknowing of what lies above us. I want as many bodies on the ground that we can afford, so it will be all five of us. Once we execute these two Exalls, we'll be hitting the road immediately. The team has agreed to keep your dad restrained in the trunk until we can figure out a way to fully cure him. We'll also bring as much of the lab materials as we can fit. That way we can keep researching, and on our way back this direction we can always stop here again to pick up anything else."

Kyle nodded. "Okay, that all works for me. When are we heading up?"

Ortiz checked his watch and pushed buttons on it to set an alarm. "In exactly one hour."

29

Chapter 29

Robert had returned to Larkwood the night prior and parked a quarter mile away from the Humvee. He used his binoculars to scout the area to see if the government cowards ever came outside to play. They never did, their vehicle sitting in isolation as the only visible object on a vast landscape of doom.

He considered storming their underground fort, but figured that was a sure recipe for his own death. While he didn't mind the prospect of dying—now that he had no one to live for—he didn't want to do so until seeing these mass murderers held accountable, preferably by his own hands. He didn't even know how many of them were hiding, let alone what kind of defense they had from their unlimited military budget.

"Play the waiting game," he whispered to himself when he woke in the morning, checking the binoculars in hopes of any changes. If they didn't step outside today, he planned on walking right up to their vehicle in the middle of the night and slashing their tires.

Some paranoid thoughts also ran through Robert's mind. Perhaps they knew he was following them and had coordinated a grand scheme to throw him off their trail. They could have switched vehicles, or caught a ride with other colleagues, all while he was parading around the airport like an idiot searching for nothing that existed. If any of this proved true, he could end up sitting in the middle of this dump for days without ever seeing any action.

Robert reclined his driver's seat, preferring to keep a low profile in case anyone else was around to spot him. He looked into the backseat and saw the canned peaches. The thought of forcefully shoveling more peaches into his mouth killed his appetite. He had done a good job of not longing for the way life used to be, but some days he just wanted bacon in the morning and a juicy burger for dinner. Now, he feared he might never get that opportunity again, his slow drip of unhappiness gradually eroding all optimism and desire to live.

He pulled out a cigarette stashed in the glove compartment, lighting it and taking the longest drag his lungs could hold, blowing it to the ceiling as he thought about the roads in life that had brought him to this point. Robert recognized the shift in his own mindset, but no longer felt any control over it. Where he used to be grateful for his life as an amateur conspiracy theorist, knowing it was the sole reason he was still alive today, he now dreaded the fact, alone in the world.

His grand vision had always been he and his son conquering the new world, having all their facts and knowledge. There were others like Robert and Gavin, groups that met twice a year to discuss their recent discoveries and plans for what they referred to as The Transition. He could only assume that most of his friends from that group were still alive today. They had no meeting place for when the world went dark, each member of the group responsible for seeing matters through in their home states.

Robert decided his time would be best spent recruiting more help from the underground society beneath Denver International Airport. From there, he and a new army of survivors would spread across the land, ramping up efforts to create a new society immediately.

Gavin's death spoiled everything. His son, his sidekick, and his only reason for wanting to see any of this through. Without him, Robert not only lacked motivation, but his mind became a scattered mess, logic and common sense slipping into a dark void. He often caught himself staring into space, imagining what life would have been like if his wife had never passed away and Gavin never moved out of state. He even imagined, occasionally, what life might have been like had he never met his wife and stayed single. Would he have still fallen into the conspiracy theory surrounding an alien species trying to overthrow the world, or would he be dead under the rubble like everyone else?

Robert wasn't much for psychology or acknowledging an abstract emotion like depression, but he could recognize the resemblance of such a state of mind after having suffered through it when his wife passed. He often kept his emotions in check, a sense of pride and masculinity, leaving him a lifeless blob sitting in a car he didn't want, in a city he no longer desired being in.

Killing the government people responsible for all of this mess would be the only thing to make him feel better, and if he had to sit in this hideout for the next month to see it through, then that's exactly what he would do.

He lifted his head for the off chance of seeing something in the distance, his eyes widening when he saw what appeared to be bodily figures roaming the area around the Humvee.

"Holy shit!" he gasped, pulling the lever that shot his seat upright, snatching the binoculars from the passenger seat. He looked into them, butterflies swirling in his stomach as it seemed fate was finally throwing him a bone. The soldiers were all outside, guns drawn as they appeared to be searching for something. They moved in a circle, backs to each other as they drifted away from the open hatch. "What the hell?"

They were an odd-looking bunch with four soldiers of all different sizes, one even appearing to be as young as a teenager. A fifth person appeared dressed in layman's clothes. *Another survivor they picked up on the way?*

The man had a rifle like the rest of the group, and knew how to hold it correctly, so it was possible he was still a fellow soldier who maybe had a wardrobe crisis. Laundry wasn't exactly a priority in this new world of simply trying to wake up the next morning. The sight of five potential soldiers made Robert's stomach sink. One against five would prove an impossible task, unless he kept a safe distance and attempted to snipe them from afar.

More concerning, however, was the distraction they caused by essentially doing a scavenger hunt. What were they looking for? And why did it prompt all of them to come out of their hideout with guns drawn?

They're not out there looking for food or supplies—not with guns. They must have a reason to think those gray bastards are in the area.

Robert panned away from the soldiers to scan the rest of the area, hoping to spot something out of the ordinary to give him a clue. He saw nothing and stepped out of the car for a better view all around. None of the soldiers appeared to have binoculars to spot him in the distance, and he wouldn't appear to their naked eyes even if he started doing jumping jacks on the rubble. As long as he remained silent, he'd have no issue staying out of harm's way.

The air felt still, but it had been that way ever since the world had fallen silent. He lowered the binoculars to confirm he was indeed far enough, seeing the soldiers appear as dotted figures along the horizon. If he could reduce the distance between them in half, he felt confident in his ability to shoot them all. He'd get to take out two of them before they realized what was going on, and possibly a third before they started firing back. If all went that smoothly, he could put himself in a two-on-one scenario where he felt much more comfortable, especially considering he had a car to run them over with.

"Now which three should I knock out first?"

30

Chapter 30

When Kyle took his first step outside, he drew a deep breath to let the fresh air coat his lungs. He had long since noticed the pureness of the air after the smoke from smoldering buildings had finally vanished, and the country had virtually no more daily pollution. It was like taking a dive in the pristine waters of a private beach, an idea that seemed ludicrous as he stared at the landscape that was once his hometown.

They had all climbed out of the bunker and immediately formed a moving circle. Major Ortiz decided it unwise to leave anyone behind. Without directly saying it, they understood they were going to survive or die together as a group, a somewhat morbidly romantic, simultaneously horrifying, thought.

"Come on out!" Ortiz howled, his voice carrying far into the distance. They covered all angles as planned, Kyle facing the bunker's open hatch as he walked backward, his father on his left.

Travis had passed the blood tests Ortiz ran, confirming that the level of Exall blood in his system was still at a manageable amount to avoid any hardships. His secret with Kyle remained on the teen's mind, leaving him ready to whip his father with his rifle should anything suddenly change. Travis still had Exall blood in his body, and that always left a door open to chaos. Whereas Kyle's controlled amount of Exall DNA left no chance of him turning on the Crew survivors, his father's situation was a completely different matter.

Kyle thought the guilt might swallow up the rest of his sanity, but the task at hand kept his mind occupied. He couldn't help but wonder, as he gazed to the open hatch, if this was part of the Exalls' plans. They could swoop in right now, close the hatch, and rummage through the bunker to uncover every secret their sworn enemy, Susan Wells, had ever kept.

Kyle shook his head, knowing Exalls weren't really interested in such matters, especially considering they were a mere knockout punch away from having no resistance. The days of mind games were over, bloodshed was the only way forward for both sides of this battle.

"How hard can it be to find two Exalls in the middle of *nowhere*?!" Bernard shouted, kicking an empty coffee can with the force of a soccer player.

"Simmer down," Ortiz said.

"They probably see us and know they have no chance of surviving," Bernard replied, still kicking the random objects that dared to lie in his path.

Camille stood on the other side of Kyle, speaking over her shoulder. "You know how patient they are—we need to be ready to wait a while for them to make a move."

They crept further away from the safety of the bunker, wondering if they had perhaps seen the last of it.

A gunshot burst, the sound echoing all around them. They stopped, everyone's heads jerking from left to right in search of the source. A second shot rang out, and Bernard dropped to the ground, blood gushing from his throat.

"Everybody down!" Ortiz barked, diving to the ground, right hand still clutched around his rifle. Kyle followed suit, shoving his father, who went tumbling forward. Kyle crawled along the ground, dodging the massive splinters of wood that stuck out of the debris.

The gunfire continued, showering over them at an alarmingly rapid pace. Dirt and rubble exploded around them as the stray bullets kept inching closer. Ortiz rolled away, arms shielding his head, Camille copying the same motion with much more grace.

Kyle caught sight of the faintest of flashes in the distance. "Over there!" Kyle shouted, crouching into a shooting position and immediately returning fire. He shot blindly into the void, hoping to at least scare off whoever was shooting at them.

Travis rolled and rejoined Kyle at his side, jumping up to his knees, where he started shooting his rifle in the same general direction as Kyle.

Voices filled Kyle's head as he continued shooting, and he tried to shake them out, to no avail. They started as soft murmurs, before growing louder, as if he were sitting in the middle of a crowded restaurant and could hear everyone's conversations around him.

"Do you hear that, Ky?!" Travis shouted from next to him, confirming Kyle's knee-jerk suspicion that the Exalls had somehow slipped through whatever barrier existed and had infiltrated Kyle's mind. And apparently his father's, too.

There had to be at least two dozen voices speaking at once, causing such a chaotic jumble of words that Kyle couldn't make out anything being said. "Stop it!" he screamed, jerking his head so violently that his neck would be stiff for the next couple of days.

"Ow! Fuck!" Ortiz cried, demanding the attention of everyone around. He writhed on the ground, hand clenched over his bicep where blood seeped out from between his fingers. "They fucking got me. Keep shooting!"

Kyle spun back around and reloaded a fresh magazine, returning to the task at hand while Camille tended to Major Ortiz.

"It's coming closer!" Travis cried, and Kyle wasn't sure if he was referring to the voices or the gunfire. Until he caught the glimmer of a car moving toward them. "They're driving at us."

"Hold your ground and keep shooting!" Kyle shouted back, confident in his ability to hit the target, growing larger by the second. Now he could make out the figure of a man hanging out the driver's side window, a pistol in one hand while the other controlled the steering wheel.

They kept shooting, the windshield shattering, the vehicle swerving as it approached. Kyle didn't know who landed the blow, but the front passenger-side tire exploded, rubber shards flying like shrapnel in every direction. Sparks flew as the wheel dragged through rubble, the car losing all control.

"Move!" Kyle howled, diving aside, catching a glimpse of his father doing the same. The vehicle, now visible as a Ford Focus, hit the slightest of dips, sending the car into a tumble as it rolled three times before coming to a complete stop a mere ten feet in front of where Kyle and Travis had just crouched. Camille had Major Ortiz sitting up, and the two watched with their jaws hanging. Ortiz still had his rifle clenched in a fist, now moving it toward the idle car.

The car sat silently, all of its windows cracked, blocking out any visibility of its inside.

"No way the driver survived that," Travis said, taking cautious steps away from the vehicle, rifle still cocked and ready.

"They can if they're not human," Kyle said, stepping forward, eyes drawn to the car, refusing to look at anything else.

The passenger door swung open, an older man tumbling out and falling to the ground with a hectic clatter, arms and legs flailing as he struggled to his feet. "You took my boy. I'll kill you all!" he shouted, reaching back into the open door.

A gunshot rang out, and the man dropped dead in an instant, falling on his back, arms whipping above his head to reveal a pistol in hand. Kyle looked over to see Camille standing tall, both hands on her pistol, as she hesitated to lower her weapon.

"Nice shot," Ortiz said, forcing a grim grin. He kept his hand clamped over his arm, a torn piece of cloth now wrapped around his wound to slow the bleeding.

Kyle made his way toward Bernard, who had been pushed to the back of his thoughts amid trying to survive this encounter. The man lay on his back, mouth wide open, eyes glazed and staring at the blue skies above. Emotions swelled within Kyle's chest, but he refused to shed a tear for his friend. Not like this.

Camille hurried over and joined Kyle, immediately throwing her hands over her mouth and turning away from the sight. "Oh, my God," she mumbled, falling to her knees

Kyle crouched down and closed Bernard's eyes with a soft brush of the fingertips, the act making him nauseous.

Major Ortiz grunted as he rose to his feet, wobbling off balance as he made his way toward the rest of the group. He labored over and stopped next to Kyle, crossing his arms and hanging his head, shaking it in disgust. "He saved all of us," Ortiz said, his voice shaky. "And we couldn't return the favor. He is literally the only reason we are not mindless Exalls right now."

Tears welled in the major's eyes, and seeing this caused the same to happen to Kyle. Travis approached and put an arm around his son.

"I tried, Major," Kyle said. "I had no idea where the shooting was coming from."

Ortiz shook his head even harder. "There is no blame to pass around, so don't bother. These things are bound to happen in this line of work—all you can hope for is that today isn't you turn." He dropped his head again and let his gaze fall to the dead body in front of him. Camille stood back up and slipped in next to Ortiz. "Thank you for always trying to put a smile on our faces," he continued. "You were a dedicated member of this organization, and I know none of us on this squad will ever let your legacy fade. You're a hero and made the world a better place.

"We must never let Bernard's death pass in vain—we have to finish the job we set out to do."

Ortiz paused and allowed for a moment of silence.

Camille cleared her throat before speaking. "What are we going to do now?"

Just as she asked this question, the ground rumbled, Bernard's body vibrating. Everyone's instinct was to cock their guns and scan the area.

"Earthquake?" Ortiz asked, rather composed.

"Afraid not," Travis said, looking to the north.

They followed his stare and saw the darkness of hundreds of figures clustered together, roughly a half mile away.

"No way in hell," Camille said to herself. "Exalls?"

"How are there so many?" Kyle asked, but he already knew. They were after him. No matter what happened in the country—or even the world—all the Exalls ever wanted was to get their revenge on Susan Wells. They were coming for one thing only, and wouldn't hesitate to kill anyone who got in their way. This was the site of Susan's house, and what sweeter way to complete their revenge by killing her only grandson on her own property.

"Goodbye, friend," Ortiz said to Bernard, crouching down to plant a kiss on his forehead before standing back up and facing the rest of the group. "We need to get back inside that bunker right now—it's our only chance."

"What about Bernard?" Camille asked. "What about the Humvee? We can leave!"

"Bunker. Now!"

31

Chapter 31

Everyone panted for breath as they scrambled to their spots in the bunker, Major Ortiz cutting the lights. "We have to keep the lights off and stay quiet," he whispered. "Some of them might see through walls, and we already know some can hear us without being in the same room."

"They brought an army," Camille said. "What the hell are we supposed to do? Why didn't we get in the truck and make a run for it?"

"We'll be safer down here. The hatch is locked and can only be broken open with heavy machinery—which doesn't exist anymore. We're safe, and just have to wait them out."

"You can't be serious," Camille snapped. "You're fine just assuming they won't get in here, but if they break that hatch, that's the end of us. Hiding in a bunker like cowards."

"I'm sorry. Are you suggesting we go out there and fight?"

"We need to *leave*. They're walking on foot, so let's get in the Humvee and drive as far away as we can."

"They obviously know we're here. Running won't do any-thing. We have the resources down here to wait a very long time. The Exalls will have no choice but to move on, and now we know how many of them there are."

"Exactly, so they can leave five of them here to wait as long as necessary for us to go back out, while the rest destroy whatever remains of this country."

Kyle hadn't jumped into the conversation, mostly because he had lain down on his bed and closed his eyes to hear what the Exalls might be saying as they marched toward them.

Ortiz and Camille continued to bicker while Kyle fell into his mental trance, Travis silent and likely doing the same thing. Nothing came through at first, but Kyle remained persistent in opening his tunnel and waiting. They were likely too far out of range for anything to be picked up, but after a couple of minutes he heard his father.

Kyle, are you in here?

Dad!

Do you hear them? I can't make out what they're saying. It sounds like a chant of some sort.

I don't hear anything yet.

Honestly, it doesn't matter. I think this is the end for us—I sense it. We can't fight all of them off.

Don't talk like that—we have weapons. We have a chance.

Maybe we do, but I'd be a fool to pass up this moment to tell you I love you, Ky. I know I've been telling you that a lot over these past few days, but I really want you to know it. Me and your mother are so proud of you. You handled everything with so much maturity, such grace—the divorce, the attack on Brian, learning about this secret life your grandmother kept hidden. Any of those could have set you on a different trajectory, but what did you do instead? Packed your bags and moved to Washington, D.C. all by yourself to start a new life. At seventeen. Regardless of what happens today, you should be proud of yourself. You've already achieved more at your age than I ever could have imagined for an entire life. You're an inspiration, and I know your mom felt the same way.

Thanks, Dad, I'm not sure what else to say—I've just been going along for the ride.

I'm sure it feels that way to you, but it's much bigger than that. You grew into a man overnight and are already a hero in my eyes. I only hope that you are equally proud of what you have achieved.

Tears welled in Kyle's closed eyes as he lay on the bed. *Of course I'm proud. And I'm grateful to have you as my dad. I learned everything from you, even if you didn't realize it. I'm the person I am because of* you. *My success is your success. I love you too.*

Silence filled the mental airwaves between the two, Kyle still unable to hear any of the approaching Exalls.

I'm glad to hear that, Travis finally said. *I'm going to try to save us.*

What do you mean? How?

Nothing but silence.

Dad?

Just stay quiet and trust me. I'll be in here with you. Just trust me. You keep trying to listen in on them.

Kyle opened his eyes and sat up, wanting a visual on his father, wondering what the hell he was going to do. Ortiz clicked on a flashlight and swung it over to Kyle, making him shield his eyes.

"Wells, were you listening to them? Pick up on anything?"

"No, sir, but it sounds like my dad could."

The flashlight spun around the room until it landed on Travis, sitting on the edge of his bed with his hands crossed on his lap, eyes closed as if in prayer.

"They're coming, Major," Travis said in a soft monotone. "And they have zero plans on leaving until they have captured us."

Kyle had no way of knowing if this was true. Just moments ago, Travis had cited an odd chant from the Exalls and mentioned nothing of substance. But it was entirely possible that he had picked up more information since then.

"Christ," Ortiz spat. "It's okay—we can still wait them out." For the first time, Kyle heard true, unabashed fear in the major's voice.

The room fell silent as the rumbles above grew louder and shook the world around them.

"How are they doing that?" Camille asked. "There's not *that* many of them."

"It's most likely a mental ability. Exalls have been known to play with the elements of the world. Or it's just a total mind game they're playing to scare us out."

The vibrations strengthened, rattling objects in the bunker, a couple of framed pictures of landscape art crashing to the ground.

"This isn't fake!" Kyle cried, retreating to his bed and squeezing his pistol, the only thing that seemed plausible at this point in the Exalls' attacks.

"Everyone get down and take cover," Ortiz shouted, hitting the ground and rolling against his bed, whipping the pillows over his head.

Kyle did the same and braced himself for a most certain death, hoping it would be quick and painless. The earthquake, or whatever it was, continued for two minutes until coming to an abrupt stop.

The bunker had become hazy from the dust rattling off the

concrete ceiling above their heads. Ortiz was the first to stand back up, brushing off the powder with his good arm, looking up and around.

"Is it done?" Camille asked, peeking out from under her covers. She had apparently accepted death in the heat of the moment and decided it best to just lay on her bed until it came for her.

"It's done, but they're up there," Travis said, eyes beaming toward the hatch. "I can *feel* them all around us."

They all followed his gaze but saw nothing, even Kyle, who had tried for a moment of focus. His dad took control of the situation by being the only one with knowledge of what was occurring outside.

"What are they doing?" Ortiz asked. "Can you see them?"

Travis shook his head, not breaking his stare from the hatch, his eyes looking *beyond* the bunker. "I can't physically see them, but they're all waiting. I can hear their chatter, but can't make out anything in particular. It's kind of like sitting in a restaurant when it all jumbles together to make white noise. They're patiently waiting and will stay as long as it takes. They know we're down here."

Camille started loading a magazine with the rounds she had kept stashed in her suitcase. She looked around the room for additional ammunition, frowning as she mumbled about having more stored in the Humvee outside.

Travis raised his hand to her. "Don't bother," he said, his voice cold and distant. He lowered his head and studied the three Crew members that remained, his son included.

Kyle stared back, trying to read his father for a look he had never once seen. It was a deep, meditative expression: eyes nearly shut, a soft jaw, but a hard furrow on his brows. Travis appeared to be reading the room, perhaps conjuring the perfect words to say as they all sat in suspense. He had total control of the room, but didn't seem to know it, biding his time. Thinking.

"Thank you all for trying to save me from this infection," Travis said, eyes wide open again. "I know it was a burden, and I would have completely understood if you left me behind." He shifted his focus to Major Ortiz. "But you didn't. That's not the Crew way—I know that from my mother. She'd be very proud of you, Major."

Ortiz nodded in appreciation, his leg bouncing out of control as his impatience sky-rocketed.

"I know it helps to be her son, and maybe that's why you helped me—but none of that matters. All my life I've understood that I'd never be enough for the Crew. I've gone through some dark periods trying to make sense of why nothing I did was ever good enough for this organization, which was an extension of my mom. I took it personally, and it beat me up mentally and emotionally. Eventually I understood it wasn't personal—the Crew has particular standards and criteria that must be met. After that, I could focus on my life with a much healthier outlook. It's been a good life."

Kyle's heart and stomach sunk in unison. The impromptu speech sounded too much like a farewell, and the unknowing of where his father was going with this drove him mad. Tears welled in Travis's eyes.

"This infection is alive and well inside of me. I don't need a blood test to know that. It's not going away, either. I can sense as much. I've started having some of the violent thoughts you've all warned me about, but they've come and gone so fast that I didn't even realize it until after the fact. The way I see it, I'm on my virtual death-bed. I have no interest in becoming an Exall, and I certainly don't want to put any of you through having to kill me."

Tears streamed in a heavier flow, his lips quivering.

"I may have never been enough on paper for the Crew, but one thing Susan Wells drilled in to me was to be ready. Ready for what, I never knew until today. I've been having visions since Sandra attacked me. I can make the world right, and I know this for a fact, but it will be my last act in this lifetime. Captain Monroe, I saw you grab those special bombs from Bernard before we came back in, and I understand there are more in here. I'd like to have them."

The room fell silent as all eyes bounced back and forth from Camille to Major Ortiz. Camille looked up, her eyes focused and steady.

"You don't have to do this, Mr. Wells," Ortiz quickly added. "There is no reason for it."

"I have my reasons, and my current fate leaves me no other options if I want to protect those I care for."

Kyle's legs grew wobbly, and he stumbled forward into his father's embrace, tears of his own streaking down his cheeks. He buried his face into Travis's chest, words impossible to speak as his throat clenched shut. Travis ran a calm hand up and down his son's back before separating to meet his glossy eyes.

"You can't," Kyle said, a near whimper. "*I* can't."

"You're going to be okay, Ky. I have all the faith in the world that as long as you live, things will always work out. You have that kind of light inside of you—something your grandmother knew the day you were born. Let me do this for you, and you can go back to making the world the beautiful place it deserves to be."

Kyle swayed, but kept his balance, realizing this was the last time he would see his father.

"I need to be going now," Travis said, hugging Kyle one last time. "There's no other way out. I only ask that you finish the work you set out to do, that way you have your whole life ahead of you and can tell your kids all about their grandfather."

Kyle couldn't see, his vision completely blurred by the liquid in his eyes. "I'll never let the world forget you, Dad."

They pulled apart, and Kyle collapsed to the floor, body trembling as his mind tried to process everything that had just unfolded.

Travis reached out a hand to Major Ortiz, who instead pulled him in for a hug. Camille made her way over, three bombs in hand.

Ortiz grabbed them first and held them out to Travis. "Through the authority vested in me as the highest-ranking official in the Crew, I'd like to welcome Travis Wells as an official member of the Crew." He handed them over, turned back to his bed and grabbed a duffel bag filled with seven more, handing it to Travis. "This should make it easier for you carry all of those."

"Thank you, Major, I really appreciate it," Travis said, the slightest of grins forcing its way through the sorrow. He looked to Kyle one more time, and they locked eyes, Travis nodding to his son before turning to climb the ladder up to the hatch, duffel bag slung over his shoulder. Ortiz trailed behind to ensure the hatch closed properly behind him. When Travis reached the top and turned the wheel to unlock it, he looked down. "I wish you all the best. See you on the other side."

He pushed open the hatch, a stream of sunlight briefly flashing into the bunker before he stepped out and closed the hatch again, drowning out the sounds of hundreds of Exall screams. They sat in silence for the next five minutes, listening to the sounds of steady explosions above, once again feeling the Earth rumble as Travis cleansed it from its grandest threat.

Chapter 32

They waited for an entire hour of uninterrupted silence before taking the chance of going outside. Kyle had sobbed himself into exhaustion once the rumblings above had stopped. His face and abdomen hurt from the crying, and they'd remain sore for the next several weeks. It was only a few months ago when he had both of his parents, his best friends, and a high school sweetheart. All of them were gone now, demolished with the rest of the country, not so much as a hair on their heads remaining for Kyle to hold on to.

Camille and Major Ortiz were literally the only people he knew now, and while the thought sickened him, he felt some comfort knowing they were also in the same situation. They still had to go to California to search for the major's family who may have survived. But the urgency—and the hope—had completely vanished whenever he spoke of that leg of the mission. Optimism had become obsolete in this new world, and Major Ortiz realized he wasn't exempt from that simple fact.

No one spoke a word during that hour in the bunker. Nothing

could be said. They hadn't yet had a moment to process and grieve the loss of Bernard, not to mention the emotional roller coaster Travis had taken them all on before sacrificing his life. Sometimes silence was the only medicine that allowed reality to come into full focus.

Neither Kyle nor Camille had noticed when Major Ortiz stood up and crossed the bunker toward the ladder. His deep voice grabbed their attention, startling them as they had fallen deep into their own thoughts.

"It's time," he said, choosing to remain in the shadows of the darkness. No one had bothered turning the lights back on—it didn't seem there was a need to. "I know this is the hardest day of this mission—possibly our lives—but we have to keep going. Travis Wells made sure that we'd be able to stay on track, and we owe it to him, to Susan, to everyone who has made this possible. I know there are more people out there. The mission hasn't changed. We need to find them and restart society. Anything less than that will make us complete failures. The fate of the future is literally in our hands."

Camille rose to her feet, energy depleted as she dragged herself toward Ortiz. "I can't believe Bernard was killed by a total stranger and not an Exall," she said. "Is this the world we're going to encounter out there? Are we going to face more danger from the surviving humans than the Exalls?"

"Of course not. We don't know what the deal with that man was—he may have even been possessed by an Exall. The people we'll encounter will be scared. Hopeless. That's where we come in."

"And just pretend everything is okay? We don't even know if there are more Exalls out there waiting for us. If only one survived, they could—"

"Enough," Ortiz said, his voice calm and soft. "We can sit here and argue about the next steps, but we will never know what is outside unless we look for ourselves. And that fact doesn't change if we wait another five minutes or five years—it will always be a gamble. We either step outside and continue our work, or end up like the rest of the population. So let's tear the Band-Aid off and see, and hope that Mr. Wells accomplished what seemed so pure in his heart."

Kyle stood. "We leave here together, and I'm ready. The major is right—it's time to keep moving. I'm going to keep looking forward and not back. My life in this town, this house, is gone. We're not even a part of history because there *is* no more history. Today is day one that some future civilization will look back on and attribute to their origins. Once we're gone, there will be no more recollection of the world before the bombs dropped. No records of the violence and hatred that plagued the human race. No wars. No pain. No memories. Even now, I understand that the moment I step out of this bunker, my life as I knew it will come to an end. My family is gone, my schools I went to are gone. All that matters is what's next."

Ortiz flicked on the lights, blinding everyone for a moment while their eyes adjusted, finally revealing red and puffy eyes for all three of them. "You're an incredible young man. I know for a fact I'd be begging to hide in here forever when I was your age."

"Maybe it's the Exall blood in me that makes me mature," Kyle said with a soft grin.

Ortiz shook his head and climbed up the ladder, looking down when he reached the top. "Are we ready to do this?"

Camille nodded and followed him, Kyle tailing behind, taking a moment to soak in his grandmother's bunker, knowing he'd never return. He had felt her presence on rare occasions since her passing, but none as intense as this moment. Whatever realm she was in, she was definitely in her bunker, perhaps also saying goodbye to it for the last time. Kyle couldn't help but feel, that through all the work and innovation Susan had achieved during her time with the Crew, *he* had been her primary mission all along. She had always shown an ability to be one step ahead. Maybe she understood this time would eventually come, and the only thing that mattered was putting Kyle and Travis in the bunker together when the moment came.

Had it played out any other way, they'd either all be dead or hiding in the bunker until they eventually starved to death.

"Let's do it," Kyle said, grabbing the bottom of the ladder, giving one last look over his shoulder. The bunker hadn't changed, minus the extra beds spread across the room. His first journey down here, an evening that would be impossible to erase from his memory, seemed like another lifetime. They did not need to go back into the lab. Research could only take them so far at this point. That room only housed horrendous memories, anyway.

"I love you, Grandma," Kyle whispered before climbing the ladder, having the urge to cry, but no more tears left to shed. He never looked back.

Major Ortiz pushed the hatch open, its joints creaking and whining as sunlight spilled inside. "No one out here," Ortiz called down, a wide grin spreading across his face.

He climbed out quicker, prompting Camille and Kyle to follow suit as they rushed out of the bunker. Kyle stepped foot on the ground and spun around for a panoramic view of his surrounding hometown. No Exall corpses remained, as they evaporated into dust upon death, but the proof lay across the ground in hundreds of piles of clothes and weapons. The silence engulfed them, not so much as the light whip of a breeze present while they stood with jaws hanging and eyes bulging.

You did it, Dad, Kyle thought, unable to contain a grin. In this moment, Kyle wasn't sure how he should feel. Of course, he mourned his father's death, but seeing what he had accomplished in his sacrifice was overwhelming, filling Kyle with pride. With all the research and preparation the Crew had put into defeating the Exalls, spanning more than half of a century, it all came down to the son of their best soldier blowing them up to save the world.

"There were a lot more than we thought," Ortiz commented, his eyes focused into the far distance where the small mounds of clothes stretched to the horizon.

"Thousands of them, you think?" Camille asked. "And he killed them all with ten bombs?"

Ortiz nodded. "Those bombs were incredibly powerful—I think more powerful than Bernard understood while creating them."

"This had to be all of them, don't you think?" Camille asked. "Thousands of Exalls coming to this place to ensure we no longer existed as a threat. They were the ones not wanting to take any chances, and it backfired."

"Bernard and my dad are the true heroes," Kyle said, brimming with joy at the sight of their accomplishments.

"That they are," Ortiz said. "I suppose other Exalls can remain elsewhere in the country, but I agree with the captain—they were all here. Every last one of them."

"Where do we go from here?" Kyle asked, planting his hands on his hips while they looked out to the landscape.

They remained for a moment, enjoying the visual of a clean

slate. Kyle thought of all the memories he had made in Larkwood and wondered if he'd ever return once the country grew into its new form. He had no reason to come back, no landmark or graves to visit. The memories were his own and would only remain in his mind and heart. His family, his friends, his old life now only existed within himself. The future would bring plenty of change and surprises, but he would always know the truth behind those who made it all possible.

Ortiz stood between Kyle and Camille, and stretched out his arms around both of them. "We still have the Humvee, so back to the road. We'll head to California and turn around back to D.C. to get started on the next leg of this mission. Rebuilding—what a beautiful new world it will be."

Free Download - A Poisoned Mind

Read a spinoff story about the Exalls for free by CLICKING HERE. Check out A Poisoned Mind today!

A POISONED
MIND
ANDRE GONZALEZ

Acknowledgments

Thank you so much for reading this series. I hadn't planned for it to be a series when I wrote the first book, but I felt there was so a lot more left to flesh out in this universe. I've come a long way since that first book, which was my very first published work. With over ten books written in between the first and the subsequent two, it may seem like two different authors wrote this series. Which, I suppose, is kind of true. I've grown and learned so much as a writer during this journey, and now publishing my fifteenth book, I finally feel comfortable with where my skill-set is. If you've been with me since the first book, I want to extend a huge thank you. Finishing this trilogy has felt like closing a chapter of my life, and I'm honored to have had you along for the ride.

I want to thank my editor, Stephanie Cohen-Perez, for once more cleaning up the manuscript. I know it wasn't easy to jump into a series you didn't originally edit, but your work has been superb in completing this series.

Thank you to Dane Low, my cover designer, for again coming up with a stellar concept.

And I can't leave without thanking my kids for always reminding me why I'm doing this. Without them, this would all just be me writing words with no purpose.

Lastly, my wife, Natasha. Thank you for handling other matters in our life to allow me the time to sit down and write.

You are the backbone of all this, and I can't wait to see where this journey continues to take us.

Andre Gonzalez

July 3, 2020–August 20, 2021

Enjoy this book?

You can make a difference!

Reviews are the most helpful tools in getting new readers for any books. I don't have the financial backing of a New York publishing house and can't afford to blast my book on billboards or bus stops.

(Not yet!)

That said, your honest review can go a long way in helping me reach new readers. If you've enjoyed this book, I'd be forever grateful if you could spend a couple minutes leaving it a review (it can be as short as you like) on the Amazon page. You can jump right to the page by clicking below:

http://mybook.to/FollowedAway

Thank you so much!

Also by Andre Gonzalez

Wealth of Time Series:
Time of Fate (#6)
Zero Hour (#5)
Keeper of Time (#4)
Bad Faith (#3)
Warm Souls (#2)
Wealth of Time (#1)
Road Runners (Short Story)
Revolution (Short Story)

Amelia Doss Series:
Salvation (#3)
Nightfall (#2)
Resurrection (#1)

Insanity Series:
The Insanity Series (Books 1-3)
Replicate (#3)
The Burden (#2)
Insanity (#1)
Erased (Prequel Short Story)

The Exalls Attacks:
Followed Away (#3)

Standalone books:

About the Author

Born in Denver, CO, Andre Gonzalez has always had a fascination with horror and the supernatural starting at a young age. He spent many nights wide-eyed and awake, his mind racing with the many images of terror he witnessed in books and movies. Ideas of his own morphed out of movies like *Halloween* and books such as *Pet Sematary* by Stephen King. These thoughts eventually made their way to paper, as he always wrote dark stories for school assignments or just for fun. Followed Home is his debut novel based off of a terrifying dream he had many years ago at the age of 12. His reading and writing of horror stories evolved into a pursuit of a career as an author, where Andre hopes to keep others awake at night with his frightening tales. The world we live in today is filled with horror stories, and he looks forward to capturing the raw emotion of these events, twisting them into new tales, and preserving a legacy in between the crisp bindings of novels.

Andre graduated from Metropolitan State University of Denver with a degree in business in 2011. During his free time, he enjoys baseball, poker, golf, and traveling the world with his family. He believes that seeing the world is the only true way to stretch the imagination by experiencing new cultures and meeting new people.

Andre still lives in Denver with his wife, Natasha, and their three kids.